The Devil Duke's Little Distraction

Darling Duchesses Book 1

Alyssa Bailey

Falling in love was never part of the bargain.

Lady Sofia Cloverfield's family has disintegrated, and she finds herself on the streets to make her own way with only a few guineas and her wits with which to rely on to survive. Sofia uses her common sense and prays she can figure out how to turn her fate around.

Exeter Trenton, the Devil Duke, is wealthy, handsome, and lonely. His position demands he take a wife, but he finds none to his liking. Then, quite by accident, his luck changes when his horses nearly trample a waif he mistakes for a child. He allows her to leave with his chastisement ringing in her ear but not before he finds she is no child.

Once home, Trenton finds he can't get the little minx out of his mind. Telling himself he would be creating a better life for her, he devises a plan to bring her home for a brief distraction.

The Duke initially intends to enjoy her attributes and teach her the thrills of being a woman with an attentive lover. One who engages in incomparable pleasures while remaining diligent in keeping her safe, but plans change, and before he can stop her, his little distraction has gotten under his skin and crawled into his heart.

Now the Devil Duke can never let her go.

Just as Sofia realizes Trenton is more dangerous than she ever suspected, her heart is engaged, and her life is at risk, forcing her to draw on every skill she has learned to save herself from a fate she had barely escaped several times before.

Trenton's goals for Sofia may have changed, but not even the confident, masterful, and influential Duke can see into the future and know that someone else has a different ending planned for his Fia… *a very different ending*.

Love the inside scoop? Sign up for my Newsletter with special offers and bonus content.
https://www.alyssabaileyromance.com

Cover Design by Pro_ebookcovers
Manufactured in the United States.

Prologue

Was it too much to ask? Sofia wondered as she gathered what few possessions, she had left to her after other residents in this house of horrors stole them. She wanted to take the small girl lying next to her, whimpering in her sleep, but Sofia couldn't. The child wasn't hers, and besides, she didn't even know where she would go. Little Myra still had her mother bless her, and that was where she needed to be.

Sofia had to suck up the pain it caused her to leave the child in such a dingy, desolate workhouse after only knowing her a snippet in time. The memory of her own mother still fresh on her mind. The child's mother was doing what she had to do to feed her little girl. She could not fault that.

Besides, Sofia was not the woman of means and position she was just a short time ago. She longed for her own child someday, but that was for a distant future with a loving husband if she could find herself back in a position of some value to find one after recent events. Survival was something she was learning didn't come easy to those without friends, money, or position.

She needed a protector now, more than ever before. Gone were her girlish dreams, like her innocent childhood. Her knight in shining armor, her prince, was no longer someone she aspired to marry. Just a good man who would overlook her relatives and the diminished state that she now existed. She closed her eyes and released the feelings of loss the best she could.

Right now, she needed to find a way out of this place. Tonight. She shivered when she thought of the new night watchman's eyes on her. The men here were lecherous, but this man seemed even worse. He was dangerous to women. Sofia instinctively knew he was evil, and when he trained his attentions on her, she trembled in terror.

Last evening, the man hired to protect the women while they slept had tried to get close to her. Luckily, someone intercepted him; but tonight, there was a gleam in the man's eye that never seemed to travel far from her. She had heard the man answer to something like Cragins, and even the name gave her chilblains. She knew, with certainty, that he had devious plans of things she couldn't even imagine. Of that, she was quite certain deep in her belly. Yes, tonight she had to get away from the abusive workers, both male and female, and that watchman.

***

Cragas openly rubbed his cock as he watched the women sleep. He worked extra to bargain for the late-night shift so that he could pick his beauties out. Most wanted that shift to sleep instead of work, but he wanted it for profit. He had enjoyed the prime choice of female companionship when he was alone with the women he grabbed before selling them to his contacts. Working at Clerkenwell Workhouse was a shit job, but once he figured out how to maneuver things so he could be alone with the women when they were most vulnerable, things looked up.

It had been a stroke of even better luck when he had run into a broker of female attributes. Cragas took his reward frequently and then sold the women to his enterprising gentleman friend. It had turned into an excellent business arrangement, and Cragas made good money. Unfortunately, he had to give up several nights a week at this shit hole to make that money.

The young girl that wandered into the house a few days ago was his newest target. She was young, pretty, and as yet unbroken by the hardness of manual labor and poverty. Yes, he hadn't had one so fresh in a long time. Tonight, he would take her before some other got to her first. He didn't even know the rassling's name, but she sure was shiny and clean.

Cragas watched as the room grew quiet. Soon he would have his reward for watching over these poor excuses for humankind. He imagined the girl's muffled screams as she tried to escape his grasp. She would thrash and fight but could not escape him. Soon, he promised himself as he watched and manhandled his dick. He was careful not to cause himself to shoot his wad yet.

First, he would have her. Then he'd take her to his associate.

Chapter 1

Lord Exeter Trenton, His Grace to most of society, the Devil Duke behind his back to those who dared, inhaled the fresh air. Casting his gaze over the newly planted field and the river, Adur was invigorating and peaceful from his fourth-story window. Something that he needed after such a long day of settling his accounts. It was the highest window in Trenton Hall, and he commandeered this view whenever he felt the weight of responsibility heavily. Such was his state of mind today. His mother had just left to return to her sister's home, but not without challenging him on his lack of success in finding a wife.

"My boy, you are the catch of the season *every* season, and still you have not settled on a wife. I think it the appropriate time you decide what is truly important and take on that normally enjoyable task of offering for the hand of some young lady before you are no longer the sweetest fruit on the tree. More receptive men can easily distract young ladies' Mamas if it is obvious their daughters are not in your line of sight because they soon tire of parading their young ladies before you."

He knew his mother was right, but it was only recently that he had thought he would like to have a wife and family. Trenton was a formidable member of the aristocracy who cared nothing for the Ton or their fickle ways. He was a shrewd businessman, an accomplished horseman, and a stern employer. He had to be. His father had been a man of great regard, and to keep up the façade of seamless transfer of authority, he must appear to prescribe to his father's way of doing things.

He must adhere to his family's moral sensibilities, but the truth was, Exeter didn't care a whit what society thought of him. He had long decided that when he married, it would be to whom he most desired. A woman who pulled at his very soul. Unfortunately, he was the first heir, and as such, had always known that the mantle of running the estate and producing heirs fell primarily on him.

That necessary station would have been filled with little fanfare had he not had certain proclivities that prevented engaging the affections of any woman with an eye to be his broodmare. While society was rife with loveless marriages, he wanted to marry for love, and if not that, then at least find one with similar appetites. One who knew how to maintain his home and his place in society with decorum and grace but who lost all semblance of propriety behind their bedroom door.

That would mean he needed his wife to be willing. Nay, begging to be put over his knee, bound to his bed, and many other delights he had found invigorating. That woman he could grow to love. She was, however, proving hard to find.

He did not care which young tittering female was the incomparable or who got the "nod" in each year's assortment of coming out misses. His very name struck fear in over-coddled young ladies' hearts. The mamas wanted him for their daughters because of his position and wealth but feared marriage to him would be too costly for their daughters' sensitivities to reside with him daily. They were likely right, for he suffered no fools.

From what he could see, most young women were raised to be precisely that- oversensitive fools. They hid their intelligence and displayed their weaknesses. They gave society what they wanted, vulnerability and pretty faces, but nothing rattling inside their brains. It truly frightened Trenton to think obligation might saddle him with one of these examples of womanhood.

What he wanted was spirit and obedience. In exchange for that precious gift, he would share everything with his bride. He would cherish her spirit and respect the gift of obedience. Her spirit would meet him under the cover at night, and her obedience would be a matter of respect and pride. The world would be her playground, and she would be his. If he could but find the woman of his dreams, the rest of society could go hang for all he cared.

Oh, he knew what many of his peers thought of him, a devil in aristocratic garb, but it was conjecture only. That suited Lord Trenton, who was the seventh Marquess of Trent on Lea. Many years ago, his great-grandfather received a Dukedom by King George II, and the title fell to Trenton recently in the wake of his father's sudden death due to a lung ailment. Now the weight of the family's heritage, past, present, and future, rested on Trenton's shoulders.

Trenton was never a rake by the truest standards. In truth, he was a bit of a recluse but wealthy as Midas. There were rumors he had women brought to him under false pretenses and then disposed of them once he had grown tired of having his wicked way with them. At first, the tales amused him, but he'd grown tired of the ever-increasing horrors he was to have bestowed on prim and proper daughters of society.

Where these tales started, he could only imagine, but in the early days, he had perpetuated them whenever he could to keep the mamas at bay. His mother said that it was mamas themselves who likely began the stories to explain why their daughters were denied his offer of marriage. Trenton rarely set the story straight in mixed company, for he wanted what he knew he couldn't have, a woman who was not afraid of him or his titles. He desired a woman who cared not for the tittle-tattle of bored old gossips, and yet, she must be a lady. A lady of quality clarified his mother. And if the tales of ill-repute did not frighten her spirited sensibilities, then he was happy to take her to wife.

Widowed women were drawn to him, and his mystery as honey attracted flies, bees, and all sorts of nuisances. But Trenton wanted a woman who would bow to him, but not without the occasionally heated discussion. Nor would he want her to submit for long. A woman who was sassy and readily risked the strap for being so mouthy excited him. One who enjoyed the bite of his leather and the ecstasy of submitting when he demanded, but to only him. One who would demand to be indulged for her compliance. Just thinking of pleasuring such a woman excited his craven member to iron.

It was unusual for a man to demand a love connection, but he did. Reason told him no woman would meet his criteria and fall in love with him. He wanted a woman who would not consider him a trophy because of his status in society. She was there because she couldn't imagine life without him, no matter his financial standings or his sadistic need to bind her to his bed and spank her plump arse.

Every year Trenton wove through the sea of damsels hoping to find one of these treasures, but the choices had almost seemed to dry up these last few years. When treated with respect, he was the kindest of men, and his friends would attest to the same. He took excellent care of his servants, and he rarely heard any complaints because Trenton excelled at running the estate he loved. He made money by doing what he was born to do, but he needed a diversion as he continued to look for an appropriate helpmate.

Trenton took up residence in his London townhome for the Season, timing it just when the gaiety was in full swing, hoping for a result. He would take care of business until his butler, Mr. Kerns, put the house to rights and answered the overabundance of invitations that greeted them upon arrival.

Once he had addressed the few pressing household issues, Trenton headed for the shipyard and the London office of his newest investment, Superior Shipping Lines. It was a shamefully pretentious name, but after doing his research and meeting up again with the other partners, he was inclined to believe they were indeed running a superior shipping company. It would complement his small merchant shipping venture in the south of Sussex on the English Channel.

As he entered the offices, Lord Ashton, a partner, was there. Trenton greeted him good-naturedly. "I wouldn't have thought you to be here on such a dreary day. Did her ladyship send you away so she could have some peace?"

Ashton's bark of laughter drew looks of surprise. However surreptitiously they were delivered, his friends always drew attention. He led Trenton outside. "No, Rosemary isn't at home today but out visiting her cousin Lady Thayer. She left in a whirlwind when she discovered her husband was not pleased with her choice of entertainment last night."

"Gambling the pin money?"

"It was more like giving it away to the needy waif of the world, the little imp. I allow her to donate to worthy causes to appease her and mandate her pin money is for herself. She would challenge me even now, after several years of marriage."

"Ah, she left to save herself the payment of the penalty."

"More likely to beg funds off her cousin, so I won't know she gave it all away."

"She's a bit of a bluestocking, I hear."

"That she is, and very pleased with the designation. On many subjects, even without formal education, her intellect is more honed than my own." Ashton said his words with indulgence and pride clearly discernable.

Trenton had gone to a gentleman's club that catered exclusively to men of a particular perspective. These men either had their women or were looking for one. Thayer had said it was more for camaraderie because none of the partners had gained their brides from exchanging information in that establishment.

"She keeps you on your toes, I see."

"And I often keep her off hers while dangling over my lap. Speaking of which, have you found any worthy prospects for your duchess?"

"No, and now I am to endure another season. But this business and several other interests I now have in London will keep me occupied when I am not required at the various gatherings."

"Surely you can choose which you go to."

"Yes, that is true, to some extent. I should not go at all if you have a breath of any prospects I might peruse."

"No, the choices are too meek and mild, having taken their mama's training to heart."

Trenton sighed. "As I have found. There is one out there, dammit, I know it. I have determined to find her this season."

"Good luck, my friend. I should finish my errands. Call on us at any time."

"Thank you, I shall."

As Trenton walked toward his carriage, a young girl scrambled from the far side of the conveyance, upsetting the matched pair of horseflesh hitched to the front.

Up jumped the pair, as synchronized as ever he had seen them. Instead of continuing to flee, the chit of a girl stopped right under their raised hooves. Trenton hollered and raced to save the child he was sure would be killed. Just as the deadly beasts' legs were descending, she came to her senses and bolted away just out of their reach.

Trenton grabbed the young lady up after he saw his coachman had gotten control of the team. She seemed unharmed.

"Are you hurt?" She shook her head.

Giving her several rough shakes, he looked over at a half-barrel flipped over, perfect for his purposes. He propped his left Hessian boot on the rim of the barrel and tossed up her thin skirts before he landed ten intense swats over her chemise that covered the seat of her sweet, plump backside. He covered her arse as well as the chemise.

Ignoring how much he enjoyed that, he intended that this little urchin clearly understood her actions nearly killed her. Trenton hauled her up and stood her in front of him. All the while, she continued to flail and spit obscenities. "What the bloody, fucking hell are you doing? You have no right to abuse me, attack me in the street you... you mongrel."

Stunned at hearing just words aimed at him and from a female, Trenton simply stared for a few seconds. However, he soon gathered his wits, pulling himself into his full six-foot-two stance, and glared at the girl in front of him. He could see she was a young woman and not a girl at all. Her eyes were almost violet, striking in her red face that proclaimed her skin to be delicate porcelain. She was underdressed, but the clothing was of excellent quality. She was a maddening puzzle that sparked his interest.

"What do you think you're doing, racing under the lethal hooves of my bloods? They would have crushed you."

"Right, you're a hero, and I am thankful. But no man touches me and not in such a violent, defiling way."

Her cheek was darkening as though she had been slapped or ran into something. Trenton readdressed whether the horses had injured her.

"I'll overlook the vile tongue because of the trauma. Where you could have heard such language, I will not explore. It looks like you were hurt. Let me take you home and explain things to your father."

A flash of sorrow showed on her face, and then it was gone. "No woman's reputation could survive that trip, Sir. I am perfectly able to find my own way."

"That would also be detrimental to your reputation."

Watching the girl, he thought she must be a maid and embarrassed, which was a pity. She had spunk and had taken his discipline without too much fuss if you ignored her flaming tongue. Which he wouldn't if she were his. Her shoes were of outstanding quality but well worn. Possibly her family had fallen on hard times.

He thought to give her some coin, but before he could reach into his pocket for his money, she had taken off. Trenton tried to call her back, to no avail. He watched the last wave of her sable brown hair flowing wildly as she rounded the corner before she was out of sight. Just as wild as the mink he had seen, mounted with the same coloring. Magnificent.

All the way home, Trenton thought of the young woman. She appeared of an age to be preparing for her coming out into society, but instead, she was running like a hoodlum along the dangerous docks of London. He should have smacked her arse harder and impressed upon her the need to stay out of that area. It wasn't safe.

Trenton couldn't get her out of his mind all night. He fell into bed, exhausted. The trip to London and the day had been quite long. His last thoughts were of the young lady and her sassy mouth spitting vulgarities at him. He smiled because it had been the most fun, the paddling and her spirited response, then he'd experienced in months.

The following week went by in a blur, and the young ladies searching for a husband began batting their eyes and speaking to him after contriving introductions. One accomplished young lady brazened enough to stand a bit too close to him, nearly rubbing up against him. Trenton retired to the back of the host's house to relieve himself, and if a friend hadn't accompanied him, there would have been a rather compromising situation that he would have had to extricate himself.

Lord Danbury, his friend since school, murmured to Trenton as they left the back of the house, "The chit has no decorum. She was sure she could trap you into appearing to compromise her. Do you have to deal with this often?"

"Often."

"I do not envy your position, old man, not at all. I would suggest bringing your own escort to these affairs. Better yet, you should find your future duchess post haste."

"Indeed."

The women were in all shapes and sizes, including the blue-tinged ones, most likely because of their too tightly cinched corsets and the wash in their hair. He wanted a woman who could wear a corset but didn't refuse him when he asked her to leave it off. He didn't see any of these hopefuls agreeing to that.

Trenton immediately thought of the woman on the dock. She wouldn't do that, wear her undergarments too tight, would she? No, she didn't seem to have been wearing one when he'd laid hands on her. Trenton shook his head in despair. He was hopeless. He needed to find himself a bit of muslin to address his needs, then he would stop perseverating on the chit with a mass of unruly locks and a saucy tongue.

Men routinely chastised their wives, but not unrelated women. And he felt sure they didn't do it while the lady lay over his thighs, undressed, with a plug firmly placed in her arse, which is how he preferred to chastise. No, he had earned his Devil Duke moniker, but not in the way society expected. The wharf waif came to his mind again. She was so slight and undernourished it bothered him. Her spirit drew him. He wondered where she was now.

By week two, Trenton had returned to the docks three times without a glimpse of the beauty. He convinced himself she didn't exist, or at least she had gotten the lesson to stay away from danger. Too bad. He had become so enamored with his idea of her, he couldn't go more than a few hours without entertaining thoughts of her.

But as they rounded the block, Trenton saw the tail end of her skirts, her flowing hair giving her away. He directed his driver in her direction, but she disappeared in the labyrinth of shops and humanity. Disheartened, he continued to his destination. But a plan was brewing.

Chapter 2

The next afternoon, Trenton put down his communication. "Kerns, I've just received notice that one of my local seasonal lots of wool is on its way to the docks to be shipped out. They haven't bagged it up yet, so I have a unique opportunity to check the quality before it is loaded. I'm going to take it."

"Yes, Your Grace. I will have your coach readied."

"Thank you, Kerns."

The butler started to leave when he turned back to speak. "Are you sure you want to send your merino wool to the Colonies? Will they appreciate the quality?"

"Oh, yes. They won't only appreciate it, but it will be in high demand because the Colonists do not have these sheep, so I am told. It is highly prized on both sides of the ocean."

Trenton's pulse kicked up a notch. Maybe he would find a glimpse of the mysterious lady that had haunted his days and nights. He had not anticipated encountering a woman that affected him like she did. He was anxiously looking forward to meeting up with the spicy young woman with a scandalous tongue.

It was a humbling and maddening experience that a girl, as young as this one must be, would capture his imagination and his attention so acutely that he had no length of time that she didn't fill his thoughts. And it was maddening.

However, when Trenton arrived at the corner of the docks, there was no sign of the young lady or his product. Trenton continued on to the business at hand. He had an excellent agent, but since Trenton was here, he did the documentation necessary to ship the goods forward and reverified the receiving information. He prayed he wasn't precipitous, and the goods would be arriving soon.

As he rounded the corner on the dock to look for his product again, he had to fight the sense of loss this trip to

London had thus far produced. Shaking off the useless doldrums usually attributed to women, he spied an impressive amount of quality wool, his wool, that sat in a large cart. They were beginning to bag the wool ready to be weighed. It had been covered with a large throw made of skins to protect it. The Duke heard his livestock master discuss the Trenton Hall product with a dock worker.

"His Grace's wool is fine Merino from the best lambs imported from France some five years ago. Who would have ever thought that France would have had such a product, but they did, and now we have it. Seems the colonies want it as well, and there is little competition there. He's a brilliant businessman and employer, is our Duke. This is the last shipment of the season. I need to hurry from here to meet his carriage."

  ***

Mmm, this was heavenly. Sofia couldn't believe the excellent luck she'd had. The driver of this cart filled with incredible, comfortable wool had stopped to go into the leather goods shop. She had no trouble climbing into the back of the wool-laden cart and making herself a small opening to breathe before cuddling down into the sinful luxury. Oh, warmth. The first genuine warmth in months. The driver returned with a long strip of leather for his reins, or so he said to the man who had joined him on the front bench.

The driver told his companion the wool was going to the Colonies. That meant a ship. Sofia was frightened of the huge floating conveyances but not as much as she was living on London's streets without protection. She lived in fear every day she woke in the tiny, cavernous space she had discovered away from everyone. She hid in plain sight, afraid someone would discover her secret place, and she would have to move. Worse, she would be harmed.

Sofia had learned harsh words and how to appear capable and rough so she could fit in. Due to her genteel upbringing, her sensibilities reviled against such crassness, but it was a different world that she now lived in. She stayed away from where she slept until dusk so she could slip into her space unnoticed.

She had gotten away from the workhouse without being seen, and she intended to continue that good fortune. Her hope was to procure some work as a maid or nanny if she could only find a way to clean up adequately enough and find a reference. For now, she knew where to find food and where to sleep. That was about all she could do. It all looked so desperately tricky from this side of her childhood home, and she felt decidedly less adult during the more trying times.

The Colonies sounded wonderful, but she knew little about them, except they did not care for the British people. Maybe she should reconsider. Besides, leaving England alone frightened her as well. Sofia had heard it was warmer in The Colonies. America, that is what the red-headed Lady had called it when she gave Sofia money to run errands for her last week. Her ladyship had described a paradise. Maybe she could find the woman again to do more errands for her. It was enough funds to feed her for several weeks and assistance like that you tried to keep close by.

The more she considered her predicament, the more she stayed wiggled down into the bundle of comfort and contemplated going to America with the wool. Maybe someone there would look upon her fondly and take her home to coddle. Food and drink, she could scavenge. She had gotten good at scrounging since her brother had run away from his dishonor. Since he had left her without any means of support. Sofia had spent over a week in the workhouse after her brother sold their family home to the next Baron in line.

The home wouldn't be their cousin's for decades, if at all, but Robert had sold it to him for the money. The title would not come to their relative until her brother Robert, the fifth Baron of Cloverfield, was dead and gone. Her cousin was considerably older than Robert, and it might never have changed hands in the cousin's lifetime.

Her relative moved in with the understanding that both inhabitants quit the premises upon his arrival. Robert took their inheritance and left the country. India, she thought she heard someone say. It didn't matter now where he had gone. He had left his only family member destitute without a backward glance. He was a blackguard of the first order, and she may genuinely hate him.

The Almshouse had been a shock to a young lady of careful upbringing, such as she. Then came the advances of the men and boys. Some were younger, but all were stronger than she was. Sofia could not stay there with the horrid conditions and the meager rations, long hours, and backbreaking work. The final straw came after narrowly escaping a trap to take her against her will, sullying the only thing she had left of value, her virtue. Sofia swore she would never return. Those few days were more than enough time to know she couldn't live like that. Better free and scrounging than a slave and still scrounging. No, America was the place for her.

The slow rocking of the cart soon lulled Sofia into the first real sleep she'd had since realizing she must leave her family home. She knew nothing at that time about survival on the streets. She had learned some hard lessons like never fall into so deep of a sleep that you cannot be awakened by the sounds around you when close. And never, never give your full trust to anyone but yourself. The disillusioned Sofia was so exhausted she didn't realize that the cart had stopped, and male voices were speaking near her.

Sofie was awoken violently by clawing rough hands wrapping around her ankles and unceremoniously dragged from the warmth of her woolen cocoon. She began kicking and hollering obscenities out of terror at first, then genuine anger. The removal became more violent, and she countered by frantically trying to fight the hand that pulled at one ankle and the other shoving her skirts up by moving up her calf. She tried but soon gave up holding down her skirt over her thighs and kicked for all she was worth. Neither effort was successful. She was finally extricated from her sanctuary and dumped, unceremoniously, on the ground, skirts a bit high up her thigh. Trenton quickly stood between his man and the girl. He wanted no man gazing at her in such a compromising situation.

The young lady yanked her skirts down while trying to pull raw wool from the hair tangled in front of her face. She remained sitting where she landed on the ground. The compromising position she was in must have dawned on the young woman, for she wrinkled her pert little nose in disgust and then despair before continuing to clean herself off with long brisk strokes of both hands now. She scrambled to her feet, standing before Trenton in complete outrage. He held his smile with a mighty effort. He could devour her in one tasty bite.

Trenton's worker moved to the side and sputtered, "Who are you? You filthy, uncivilized bit of muslin. You have soiled His Grace's wool and –"

Sofia turned to face the man with a very unladylike expression of outrage mixed with incredulity to the workman in front of her. "How dare you speak to me in that manner. Spoil his wool? It is raw, uncleaned wool. I have not been the source of the dirt."

Trenton was surprised that the waif spoke with clear, cold precision as though she were a Lady of Quality, but her appearance belied any possibility of that circumstance being a reality. His Grace opened his mouth to speak to the two when she turned to center her gaze squarely on him.

"You are uncouth, sir, and your man is more so." The servant grabbed her arm harshly, yanking her away from the Duke, but Sofia continued her chastisement. "A gentleman would not allow a lady to be treated in such a manner. You, Sir, are a bounder and no gentleman."

Her voice was haughty and condemning and something else, laced with fear. It was bravado but very well executed. The woman was standing in front of a Peer of the Realm, seemingly unaffected, and dared speak to Trenton using that tone. And Trenton loved it. He wanted to hold her, protect her, chastise her, spoil her, but why? Now was not the time to dissect his desires, if ever. He was made this way, and he was tired of ignoring it.

He wanted to take the little she-devil home immediately and see what he could do to incite her ire again before taking her over his knee for a sound spanking in response to her insolence. He would likely bring her to tears before taking her to his bed if she were old enough. He would make her scream in ecstasy.

Unfortunately, he had to rebuke her for speaking in such a familiar and foal way. He was a Duke, after all. He swallowed his grin and tried to sound offended. He gave her a cursory bow in acknowledgment of her words and opened his mouth again to speak when a large, meaty hand flew through the air and landed on the young woman's face.

It was so heavily administered that it knocked the poor child to the ground. This time she didn't get up, spewing her anger. She stayed down, trying to orient herself and likely trying to stop from passing out. That concerned him far more than anything she might have done in response to her ire.

"Ye'll not speak to His Grace in that manner. Ye'll show respect."

Waterson raised his hand again, preparing to strike her once more when his hand was stayed by Trenton, who was now blazingly angry at his herder and himself. Trenton landed his fist, which seemed to move of its own volition, on his employee's jaw, then quickly squatted beside the young lady. She flinched.

"Shh, my dear. I won't harm you. You poor thing. Let me look." He spoke tenderly as if he were speaking to a skittish mare. "No one will harm you. I'm going to touch you so that I can help you stand. Are you ready?" She nodded.

He carefully helped the battered woman to her feet. His chest ached with the need to protect her. His ire at the attack was nearly uncontrollable. He forced himself to breathe slower as he steadied the young woman, delighted she matched her breathing rate to his. Dirty though the urchin was, he held her close, hugging the girl to him tightly before releasing her to see the harm.

"Are you feeling steadier?" She nodded and sniffed.

Finding she was shaken but without permanent damage, he placed his hand on the nape of her neck and lightly massaged. She stood still as a kitten when held by the scruff, and he could have sworn she hummed almost like a purr. He dared not tangle his fingers in her hair as much as he wanted to because they were too familiar already while standing in public. Trenton turned to his offended stockman.

"You never strike a woman above the full of the arse, man. Have you not learned how to treat a lady?"

Waterson's cheeks were bright red with the reprimand and the solid right hook his employer had landed on his chin, raising his righteous indignation. He was protecting the name of His Grace, after all. Trenton understood the feelings that Waterson likely was having. He imagined his stockman thought the girl was nothing but a cur that had hitched a ride in his employer's wool.

"A lady, Your Grace?"

"Yes, a lady. This one, in particular, Waterson." Trenton nodded forcefully in Sofia's direction as he continued to comfort her with his hand, now lightly massaging the small of her back just above the camber of her arse.

The Duke was typically a hard taskmaster when it came to labor. The man could have expected the punishment was deserved because the young Lady was in the wool, but the worker was inappropriately harsh. Now, at least with a woman, Waterson knew better. Waterson murmured his apologies to the Duke gruffly, not looking at their female troublemaker.

Trenton turned to the cute as hell but naughtier than was seemly, young woman. His loins ached. Now to deal with the adorable hideaway. The way he wanted to handle her was inappropriate, yet she drew him in like a siren. Bloody hell, this was complicated.

***

Sofia melted in the Duke's hold. He smelled so good and reminded her of the days, not too long ago, when she was a young lady of leisure rather than a woman who tried to hide her identity and age. The younger she could portray herself, the safer she was. Then reality had finally set in. That comfort and security of merely two months ago was not her life any longer, nor would it ever be again. She must stop torturing herself with the dream of being cared for by a lord. She may have been born to that life; however, it was folly to hope for it now.

Gaining her courage and telling herself that this Duke wasn't showing her chivalry or protection but more likely enjoying his frontal parts pushed up tightly against hers, she tried to move. She had heard of men like that. Sofia shoved against him, hard, then harder still. When he didn't release his hold on her immediately, Sofia struggled within his grasp. He tightened his hold on her nape, and she instinctively stopped.

His breath was hot on her cheek as he leaned down closer to her. "Do not be naughty, or Papa will have to spank you, and you already hurt. Don't make Papa do that. Settle down."

She dissolved into another puddle of goo. Damn him. Just when she found her presence of mind again, he said something that scrambled everything with fresh emotions. Sofia wanted to snuggle in close to this man, who was quite a bit taller and broader than she was, with his protective hold on her. When she relaxed, he rubbed her back, and she wanted to bask in his attention.

She listened to his conversation with the cruel one. The Duke had landed his fist on the man's jaw. She'd never actually seen that happen before, and she sighed at the confusing way that made her feel all mushy inside. This Duke's behavior was perplexing. He wanted to spank her and protect her at the same time? Preposterous, and yet, didn't she want that? Hadn't she realized she had always wanted that but couldn't name it?

Sofia tried to focus her mind on gaining her freedom. These feelings were frightening. Almost as frightening as being on her own. No, not that scary. But she instinctively knew that if she stayed too long, something she couldn't stop might happen. She tried to kick him but ended up in a pathetic tangle of his arm and chest, holding her upper body still while her lower body tried to make contact with his.

"Shh..." His hold never loosened. "You will do yourself harm." She struggled almost desperately now. "Calm, little one." His tone was gentle, yet he held the control with an iron hand. His other hand made a hard landing on her backside. Then another. Her movements stilled.

"I told you to do as I said. Do not push me to put you over my knee. You will be sorry, little one. Now, let's get you home."

Her jaw ached, her heart bounded hard, and she had an odd tingling deep in her lower belly. Now her arse ached as well. In her confusion of throbbing parts, she threw all her weight against the Duke and without notice, he released her. To add insult to injury, Sofia ended on her bum sitting in the dirt again. This time, the Duke never moved when she landed. She quickly scrambled up from the ground and stumbled back further from the man whose mere presence was playing havoc with her mind and body.

"You intend on making that thrashing happen right here in public, I see."

"You stay away from me, you, you…"

"The word you seek had better be Your Grace, young lady, or I will have something to say about it, and it looks like you have had enough for the evening. My strap will be talking more than my lips, I can assure you. Now let Papa help you up so we may go home."

His voice wasn't harsh, but it was firmly adamant, and her lower region tingled even more. It was a strange place to respond to what was an autocratic edict. Her body's reactions were frightening, and he was so alluring. But no, she had to get away from him and his hypnotic powers over her.

"A duke. Well, I daresay you have plenty to kowtow to you, Sir, and I shan't add to the list." She once again shook out her skirts to hide her utter revolt and chaos warring within her.

"You are a disrespectful child. Do you need another taste of my discipline? I would think you have had enough excitement, my little one, but if you need more, I will accommodate you."

There was no softness in his tone now. No protection, just pure irritation. Sofia was drawn to this man. She was appalled at her need to be near him, even in his crossness. To feel his arms around her again. She wished she could see more of him, learn about him, but that would be impossible. He was a duke, and she was a lady that had lost her status. Sofia swallowed and sniffed her tears before she spoke.

"I am no one's little one."

Her whole being belied her words, cried out in anguish that she needed to be cared for, protected, loved. But the truth of her words could not be denied. She was to be no one's little one or beloved, nor could she dream it into existence.

"I need none of your assistance in any way." Sofia looked up into an enigmatic expression that was somewhere between longing, tenderness, and control. She wanted it all aimed at her. "Sir, Your Grace, I am sorry for having caused your delay. My only intention was to find some warmth. If you don't mind, I shall be on my way."

"Actually, I do mind. I demand compensation for the soiling of my wool. I require five days from you."

"Doing what?" she had spit back that question, implying she would consider the correct answer, which she would not. Would she?

Sofia calculated how fit the two men in front of her were if she needed to run. The worker was stout but older, and the Duke? He was fit indeed, but his clothing would hinder his movement greatly. Deciding she could get away, she waited for the answer.

"Doing as I desire. I won't touch your virtue if indeed you have any, but I will require you to do my bidding. When I do not require your company, you may do whatever you desire indoors. Outdoors you must be accompanied."

"I will have you know, sir, that my virtue is intact," Sofia said proudly and then was appalled at her discussion of something so incredibly private. He smiled, and his face transformed into something magical. *Do not divert, Sofia.* She wouldn't.

"Yes, well, that is admirable, I'm sure, but I care not for your maidenhead, as I stated. Nor am I inclined to care how you pass your days." It was all a lie. He cared very much how she spent her days. And nights. "I am bored, and you have provided entertainment. I shall require those things that offer a pause in my busy day. And you shall provide them. You make me smile, and I require that of you."

"And I do what I please when I please. I am no one's jester. Accosting me, holding me down against my wishes, exposing me and reddening my backside is what you deem entertainment, sir?"

Trenton smiled. "Indeed."

What could she say to that? Certainly not that it had made her feel funny, achy for the first time in her life. Had she hurt herself and not know it? There were whispers of naughty things a young lady felt "down there" when she was attracted to a man, but surely this feeling was due to an injury when the servant had hit her for those types of things only happened to a woman who was married.

What a scandal that would be! Ladies did not have bodies that did such things, of that, she was sure. Not that there wasn't a thrill in fighting his hold, knowing he had her well and truly caught. And even the smack to her backside was notable in her lower regions. But her mind said those were oddities, not to be admired nor repeated. Her heart and body said something different.

"I am sure Your Grace will understand if I decline the invitation of such peculiarities. I am not the entertainer you seek. Good day."

Sofia turned with aplomb and ran for all she was worth to put distance between herself and the man she yearned for with all her inexperienced heart. She heard a shout and some colorful language spouted from the Duke's man, but soon, that stopped. She kept running until she found the hidden place where she could be safe for the evening. Sofia sat until her breathing calmed.

The cold began to seep back into her bones as she huddled in the makeshift hole, allowing the tears to silently trace down her cheeks. She pulled the coveted dirty quilt over herself and tried not to sniff the stench. She had brought it with her from her bed, and had it not been for its thickness, she would have absolutely frozen to death by now.

Sofia lay thinking of her Duke and tried to imagine what life would be like with a man who spanked her for insolence and hugged her for comfort. Someone who had the position to protect her and back up his protection with substance. Thanks to her brother, parents and her cousin, her life was a complete desolation with no way out. More tears flowed.

Chapter 3

Invigorated, Trenton rode home in his carriage. The little wench had innocently toyed with him. His cock was as spontaneously hard as he had seen it in a while. Was she as innocent as she seemed? As he thought of the insolence of the dirt-smudged chit, he stroked his member and reviewed the meeting. The young lady had not responded with any calculation or intent except to get in a few good jabs.

It wasn't simply that she had excited his libido, for that was not difficult in a well-appointed room with a beautiful woman, but she had stimulated his mind, thereby making his arousal massive. His entire being was sizzling with the thrill of anticipation. And something else. She had pride and a sense of morality he admired. This girl was spicy and exotic in her own way. She was a wild cat escaped from some palace wall, of that, he was sure. His little storm cloud had been raised well but no longer lived a pampered life, and Trenton wanted to know why.

The hellcat had declined his repayment option and exited from his presence quickly. It annoyed him because he wanted her to accept, but he would never force a woman to do his bidding. That excluded his servants, and even then, he rarely asked anything of them outside their duties. Trenton couldn't get the girl out of his mind nor the violence she had endured at the hands of his servant. He had to find her, purge her from his mind without compromising either of them.

Throughout the following days, the young lady continued to dog his every waking and now sleeping moment. He found the sound of her voice riding beside him across the countryside and challenging him while working his accounts. It was maddening and life-consuming and damned exhilarating. He needed to bring her home. He must bring her home. He needed a plan.

Trenton worked out different ways to convince her that it would be for a short time. Unconventional, yes. Against social norms, absolutely, but if he could entice her, they would both benefit. Trenton would make sure of that.

She was a conundrum, but the girl was of age, most assuredly. He had to look closer, but he was positive she was at least eighteen. A young eighteen in some ways, but in others... Trenton shook his head. Her recent taste of a harsh existence had begun to teach the waif the more brutal facts of life, and it showed in her forays into hooligan behavior. It was recent, for she still held unconscious mannerisms that bespoke of her upbringing.

Trenton didn't want to soil her innocence further, but he rationalized that if she stayed at the mercies of the ruffians she was surrounded by now, there would be no hope for her. The girl must not have been too long in her present situation because of her still prideful speech, but her lack of deference to himself indicated something different. That meant she had to have some socially acceptable background, but her spirit was not broken. Who knew how long she was made to fend for herself and how long she would survive? Trenton couldn't imagine such a fate for her.

He said the same of his friend Lord Thayer later that next afternoon when he stopped in to extend a dinner invitation.

"I know it's short notice but, what can I say," apologized Thayer. "Occasionally inappropriate impulsivity is part of the allowances one must make when you have a wife who is also prone to enjoy being your young lady. If you have plans, please continue with them. It would serve to help instruct Leesie that one must plan more than a few hours ahead. However, if you are available," his indulgent smile ghosted the corner of his mouth, "I don't want her too disappointed."

Lord Thayer spoke matter-of-factly, but his mannerisms were of an indulgent lover, and Trenton admired the ease with which he had integrated his desires and his wife into his high-profile life. Thayer adored his wife, that was plain to see, and he did not lose one iota of dignity by indulging her. Trenton's life was beginning to become more high profile. Now that he was determined to find a wife, he often worried his particular desires would need to stay hidden from even the woman he eventually wed.

Watching Thayer, it didn't appear to have hindered him at all, and Trenton's inclinations were no more varied than Thayer's. Besides, he wasn't going to marry the tasty morsel from the docks. And thoughts of his waif had infiltrated even a conversation with a friend. He was smitten.

"I have no prior engagement. The diversion would be perfect. I'm in a knot with this doc waif always on my mind."

"Ah, I remember those days. Now, tell me what has already transpired. I'll add my reflections at the end."

Trenton obliged. It felt good to share his confusing feelings concerning this little one. He stopped short of declaring his deepest emotions concerning her, for he expected those were infatuations that came with enjoyment and would soon fade into oblivion once he had grown tired of her antics. If he did.

"So, is it merely entertainment you seek? Or do you wish a deeper alliance?"

"With the little urchin? No. I think if I keep her with me for a sennight. A fortnight at best, I will purge her from my system and find her a more suitable lifestyle than the one she is living. A maid or maybe a lady's companion. Mother had mentioned she needed a young lady's companionship to keep her spry."

"I see. I don't advocate using the girl for a mistress. Not in your own home. It would become difficult quickly, and she would have no experience in remaining unattached. I wouldn't dally with her feelings or society's sensibilities until you have given her a respectable position in your home."

"Marriage?"

"Of course, that would be ideal for both of you, but do not take her innocence outside of marriage. It would be a cruelty to her." Thayer leaned forward in his seat. "I believe you should take her for a few weeks as a visitor, but if you desire her to stay longer, you should inquire about her exact age. If she is under 25, which I expect, becoming your ward will raise no eyebrows. It would serve two purposes. One, her reputation and yours would remain intact. Two, if you desire a deeper alliance, you have the authority to keep all others away."

"Clever. But would the courts even allow such an alliance? She has no funds that need managing." Trenton was flicking his crystal glass with his finger. The light tinging sound went unnoticed by the men.

Thayer shrugged. "True enough, but if you must find a social designation, that one will suffice. Besides, how do you know that she wasn't put out because she was in the way of someone else inheriting? You did say you are sure she had been brought up genteelly."

"There is little doubt of her upbringing, and you have brought up one possible but vile reason why she is not in a proper home. I'll consider petitioning the court if the need arises, but I tell you, she attracts me merely because I have not found a lady that arouses my affections. I am quite sure when I do, my attentions will go elsewhere."

Trenton did not sound nor feel hopeful of that happening. He feared he was already too taken with the insolent beauty to let her go.

"Then I say you have a plan. I do challenge you to take a hard look at what you really want. This appears to be an unusual alliance, and she has not been far from your thoughts since finding her. However, if you do turn the little one out after a short time, let me offer our assistance. We can take her in, assuming the miss is appropriate enough, and help her find a position."

"Thank you for the offer. I will keep it in mind." Trenton rubbed the back of his neck at the complexity of his life since meeting the young lady in question.

"There is one angle not yet addressed." Thayer finished his scotch and leaned back in his chair.

"Is there?"

"Does the girl have any living family?"

"Family? I hadn't considered that she did, given her ability to wander the streets of London as she does. If she did, she would still be in a decent home unless something nefarious is afoot."

"Remember that if she lives rough, then she isn't likely to have a person who cares, but parents may still exist."

"And if that is the case, should I inquire of the parents? I have to say I'm not inclined to do that." Trenton declared.

"I wouldn't think so. What is the girl's name, anyway?"

"I've no clue."

"Well, that is a matter you need to address at your next meeting. Anyway, she is an adult, and as such, you would be able to simply get her permission. You do intend to gain her permission, do you not?"

Thayer's tone left Trenton with the understanding that nothing less would be acceptable. Regardless of whether Trenton wished to wait for her acceptance or not, it was expected that he did wait. Her agreement was non-negotiable. Fortunately, he agreed.

"Naturally."

"Excellent. Now do not keep the little Lady hidden from your friends. Bring her to visit with Annalise and the other women once she is in residence." Thayer studied Trenton for a moment. "Regardless of her state of social graces."

"Yes, that would be perfect." *Now, to catch the minx.*

Chapter 4

Trenton snagged two pastries from breakfast. He hoped these would entice the young lady. His plan was to sit in the same place he had encountered her twice before, and when she came round, as he expected she did daily about the time he found her before, then he would have the delicacies for her.

Thayer was right. He didn't even know her name, which would be a great help in speaking to her. Trenton coached himself on his manner and his delivery. When she took the treats he offered, he would coax her home with him. It shouldn't be a difficult task.

Armed with the sweets, made with flaky, buttery pastry layers filled with heavy creamy custard and fruit, Trenton headed for the best spot to see her. He began planning everything he would do as she challenged him and pushed him to banter with her. He would edge her behavior just enough that she stumbled over the boundaries of etiquette, and he would be honor-bound to pull her back into the acceptable territory.

Not that he cared about her behavior in society's eyes, but teasing her, learning about her, and yes, even holding her tightly after spanking her sweet arse excited him. It was depraved to want her to be naughty so that he could spank her, but there it was. He was well-tagged the Devil Duke. His cock twitched at the thought of her well-shaped arse over his thighs, waiting for his hand to kiss it. And then to hold her close, kissing a new ache, he would satisfy as well.

On Trenton's first attempt, the results were not as he had hoped. Armed with his two pastries, Trenton sat as patiently as he could in a visually strategic spot for spying her but hidden enough not to easily be spied and identified by others. His intention was to have his crest mounted on this newer conveyance, but he had yet to have it done and was now glad for the delay. He watched for the little chit to make her rounds, but after several hours without joy, he decided this was a waste of time.

Where else could he go to find the girl? The mere thought that he might not see her again, stand close to her, nor be able to enact his plan to enjoy her company as he purged her hold on his sensibilities was unacceptable. There must be a way.

Trenton sat in his coach on day two to remain unexposed to the riffraff that inhabited the docks and strategized. Where was the chit? Ultimately, he decided his methods were all wrong. This was not the way to catch the girl. He needed to *search* for her. In his carriage, he was essentially sitting as in a blind, like one did when shooting pheasant. It was ridiculous.

This girl was like a young deer. Trenton must employ stealth when hunting deer and this little wild creature. The deer would not readily come to you to be taken as your dinner. Nor would this beauty, for he had determined she was just that under her sun-exposed skin and her smudges of dirt and uncleaned hair. A diamond in the rough.

After staying a while longer, Trenton returned home with a better plan for the next day. His determination had increased, and the thrill of the hunt had invigorated him. It was his intellect against her wit and wile. He intended to win the contest and take home his prize. And in the back of his mind, the part he tried to ignore, was the whisper that she would stay.

That night, he found himself smartly dressed and standing with his partners and friends as they perused the dance floor for a suitable prospect for Trenton. His heart was no longer in the chase if it ever had been. He surveyed the room but could not find anyone to slow his perusal.

"I must admit, I do not miss this necessity when single and in search of a mate," said Kendrick. "Of course, I was already acquainted with Genevieve when circumstances presented themselves, and my hand was forced. I do not regret the outcome, but the journey might have been more genteel." He allowed a slight grin in remembrance.

The others nodded and smiled. Thayer took a sip of his punch. "I do remember when you mentioned the predicament." Thayer lowered his voice. "We had to save your lady from certain, forced and yet nearly irreversible actions."

"Yes, and we were glad to help stop the unthinkable. And for Rosemary, I was infatuated immediately but was more than relieved that she was Thayer's relation. It meant she would be safe until things worked themselves out."

"Yes," said Trenton, "Did you say she was from the Colonies?"

"She's a Thayer, born on Thayer's own property, but her father took Rosemary and her mother to Virginia in the Colonies. Excuse me, America, or United States. Rosemary is quite insistent that I do not refer to them in any other way."

Colin, otherwise known as the Black Laird, grunted. "She and my Cairistine were good at finding trouble. I skelped my woman so often in the first year, I feared my hand would fall off from overuse."

"But Cairistine did help my Rosemary with the English proprieties and the formal way of doing things. She still doesn't always follow the rules, but I am satisfied that she is happy." Ashton drained his glass.

"Now, what news of your little distraction, Trenton?"

"No news, I fear. However, I do think my first expectation was unrealistic. She will not come to me, so I will have to go to her."

Kendrick drained his glass of punch. "This is a hideous beverage." His mock shudder punctuated his dislike. "Do you know where she is?"

"I do not, except I can narrow the field to the area between the leather shop several streets over from the dock she was on and the central docks."

The Laird nodded. "Is that not the area your Annalise and her brother came from?"

Thayer nodded. "It is. In fact, it was when I was visiting the leather shop that I found her outside. A fast tongue she had and still sports one today only with more decorum than her earlier days. I do still have to rein her in at times, but often it is because she desires my attention."

"Yes, but it was that sassiness that drew you to make her your wife," said Kendrick.

"Absolutely. Just as I think this chit of Trenton's draws him in with her wit and intelligence."

Trenton added, "And her sweet arse when I laid my hand to it."

The men murmured their approval. "Yes, that is a determining factor for sure. I believe we can all relate to that," said Ashton.

"And so tomorrow, I won't sit in a blind, so to speak, I go hunting for my little distraction."

"Happy hunting, Your Grace," said the Laird. "Bring food and a blanket. Our women like to snuggle in warmth and eat when they are in distress. I believe this one may entice you to keep her."

"That isn't my goal, but it is excellent advice. Now, could I interest you gentlemen in a taste of a bit more palatable drink before you must give your wives some attention?" He reached into his inner pocket. "I require fortification before I must cast a final eye over the choices for this evening."

Trenton's offer was gladly accepted.

***

Sofia woke the next morning early. She could hear only light noise outside her hiding spot and knew daybreak would come soon. It was May, and the days were warming. She didn't find herself half shivering as much even a month ago. The Duke's face came to her, unbidden, and once she thought of him, she couldn't stop her automatic remembrance of their two encounters.

There was a giddiness that came over her when she thought of him. His hand was well-shaped and slender but still significant. She wondered if he played the piano, for his hands were made for it. She had the feeling something good was going to happen today. She would see if he was near the docks later today.

Once decided, she almost skipped to her destination. She had hidden that tendency to seek out a strong man when introduced to young men. She simply couldn't abide too gentle or too disregarding, although that was all the rage these days. Not like the Duke. He was everything she had ever wanted and likely more besides. Come mid-afternoon, Sofia began looking for him amongst the hustle of the docks.

***

Trenton, determined to find his lost little lady, came better prepared. After several hours of wandering and watching, he was relieved to finally have located her. She was trying to melt into the scenery, and Trenton didn't blame her. He had become more worried for her safety the longer he searched for her. The roughness of this environment was no place for a female, never mind his spitfire.

Subduing his urge to take the girl away from this filth and degradation, against her will, if need be, he restrained himself. His protective instinct was hard to resist. Trenton wanted to take her home, away from the dangerously harsh world she resided in. But he would not force her.

Walking up beside her as she watched a young man with questionable values slowly leave her vicinity, Trenton approached cautiously. At first, she was startled and made to leave, but he spoke quickly.

"Please do not run. I know our first encounters were unwelcomed, but I would like to change that. Can we sit in my carriage? It would be safer."

Trenton tried to hide his horror at the bruise on the delicate girl's face. Was that from the wool incident?

When Sofia showed a hesitancy to follow him to his carriage, he continued with another offer. "If not the comfort of the carriage, here, on that stone wall would suffice. I simply want to make sure you harbor no lingering harm from our last encounter and to give you the pastries my cook has made. If possible, I'd like to learn about you." He pulled the pastries from his inner pocket.

"Yes, that would be agreeable." She looked longingly at the cloth in his hand. "I have not had pastries in mo… a while. Is it tender and flaky?"

He nodded and placed his hand in the small of her back to usher her to the stone wall. "Taste them for yourself."

Sofia nodded her approval. "Yes, we can sit here. I have a good vantage point in case we are besieged by thieves."

"Are you often made concerned by thieves?"

"Is that an honest question? Have you not taken the time to look around you, Your Grace? Thieves are more prevalent here than those of your breed and stature. I assure you that at this moment, you are drawing great interest."

"Yes, I imagine that to be true. Do you think I am a target?"

"To take your fine things and all the money you have on your person, of course."

"It's good that I have brought assistance then." He indicated his burly driver and his Tiger. "Is that your intention? To take what you can?"

She jumped up from her perch. "I would never take from you, but if that is what you think of me, then so be it. I don't want your pastries or you."

Trenton put out his hand quickly to stay her movements. "Please don't go. I have offended you, and it was not my intent or rather, I was interested in your response. Thank you for your kindness in sharing my company while you indulge in the sweets. Here, take this one. It is raspberry and quite good."

The temptation was too great. Taking the delicacy from his hand, Sofia sunk her teeth into the tender layers of butter and fruit. The small moan of happiness went straight to his gut, ricocheting to his heart and groin. Trenton had never been so ignited by a woman eating as he was now. She was driving him mad, and she didn't even know it. She was a danger indeed.

As she enjoyed the sweet bread, he waited and watched her face. Like a child who had been given a treat they had waited so long for, she took quick bites but chewed slowly. The entire morsel was in her mouth in a few bites, and then the ambrosia was gone. Her sadness at the end of her sweet was adorable. She declined his handkerchief and instead licked every lingering taste from the surface of her fingers.

"I wondered if you might allow me to renew my offer to have you come and stay with me for a short time. I am sure that you would be happy to be out of the weather and sleep in a safe environment once again. And it would please me to offer that to you."

"Why?" She licked her fingers, and he nearly groaned at the ungentlemanly thought that raced through his mind.

"Why extend the invitation or why you?"

"Yes."

"Could I have your name before I continue my thoughts? My name is Trenton. Lord Exeter Randolph Trenton, Duke of Trenton. What shall I call you?"

"The Devil Duke?" she barked a laugh but did not attempt to leave her spot. "You are the Devil Duke? I had thought a man of your reputation to eat little children for breakfast."

"If that were so, you would be in grave danger," he answered dryly. "How is it that you know that unflattering moniker?"

"Everyone knows it. You are said to be a terror of a man who stops at nothing and no one to get what you want."

"Ah, yes, I am well aware of the fear I am to strike in the hearts of women. The child aspect is new, however. Do you see that man before you?"

"I don't see the devil, no, but I do see a man who likes to have his way. Such as the spanking of ladies for slights they did not know they were engaged in."

"I see. Are you saying you did not know that being careless and nearly getting yourself killed was not a reason to roast your rear position?"

"My rear… oh, yes. Well, for a child, I can see that being acceptable, but I am a full-grown woman and you, sir, are not my husband."

"Yes, we do agree on your adult status, but I also believe that if a woman in your company does something so hare-brained as to nearly die under the hooves of horses, then they have earned the chastisement. And you must agree, sleeping in my wool was not appropriate."

"In your eyes, maybe, but in mine, it was an ingenious place to sleep. I would not hesitate to do so again."

"We will debate that another day, I daresay. Now I have another pastry if you have a name to share."

Sofia thought about the consequences of sharing her actual name to a man so well situated that he could have her removed from here or anywhere. Even sent to an almshouse or have his wicked way with her, both he might think perfectly appropriate. She didn't tell him what else she had heard about him. Eating children for breakfast was tame compared to the other tales. Some she didn't even understand.

If she went to his home, would the devil he was named after reappear, making the existence she currently lived become something more sinister? Would he do unspeakable things to her as rumor said he did to other women? And why did that both frighten and intrigue her?

Sofia sat quietly, contemplating her next answer, and deciding what type of man she was honestly dealing with. Her experience with men was limited as any young woman's would be, but she was surprisingly confident that she did not feel in the least frightened of the Devil Duke, regardless of his dubious reputation. Nor did she feel that Trenton had anything but a charity heart towards her, yet telling her name was intimate. Personal. It was as if she were opening the door to her soul if she gave him her identity, no matter how slight an opening.

"Fia."

"Fia? Is that short for a proper name?"

"Should it be?"

"Shall I call you Fia?"

She thought a moment, then nodded. "I think I would like that."

"So be it, Lady Fia, here is your second treat, a tart in a pastry. I'm not sure what they are called, but I think you will like it."

Once again, Sofia sunk her teeth into the heavenly sweet bread and sighed. She listened to the Duke as he discussed his offer further. "Once we have spent time together, if you want to leave the house, you may, but I would like to make sure you go where it is safe. You can choose something genteel for your livelihood. My intention is that you don't return to this place nor any like it."

"You would sell me?" Her alarm was immediate.

"Sell you? Why would I ever, oh, because I am known as the Devil, you believe me to do such things. I can assure you that I am not inclined to engage in the female trade business."

"There are those who do." Sofia's whispered words were testament to her fear at that knowledge. "In those ships that you spoke of."

"How would you know of such… Good God, do not say you have personal knowledge."

He was appalled, it was written all over his face and proclaimed loudly in his tone, and yet, it was followed by a fierceness as though he would protect her from such aberrant behavior. Again she equated him with a protector, not a fantasy she could indulge. Sofia tried to lighten things by teasing him, although it was a lame effort.

She shook her head adamantly. "No, I don't have any experience. But you are the Devil Duke." Her confusion was genuine.

"Remember, it would enhance my reputation but ruin yours if there were any hint of impropriety, and still, the mere thought is abhorrent to me." He reached out and touched her dirty hair. "I would not risk that scandal with one so lovely as you. Besides," he said in a conspiratorial whisper, "That is not where the nickname came from. It was from acts much more shocking than selling young girls."

She nearly snorted. "Now I know you are spinning Banbury tales. I am not lovely when I am unclean and unkempt. I have not properly washed my hair or myself in months. And what could be worse for a woman than to be kidnapped and sold? I know that you are not to be trusted now. Besides, regardless of what is said about you, I would swear you were an honorable man."

His voice firmed just enough to gain her attention. She remembered her father doing just that thing to stop her from going off on a tangent. But her father never made her shiver in anticipation like the Duke did.

"I do not speak of your outer appearance. Although a bath would transform your skin, it's what's inside that counts. I've enjoyed my time with you, but I have another engagement and must be leaving. Are you coming with me?" He put out his hand.

"You just want to help, but I cannot believe it is true." She wanted to go, but it was too good to be true. This handsome man could not want her to stay with him.

He spoke quietly into her thinking. "I cannot seem to stop worrying about you. You find a way into my every thought. I want to see if I can purge you from my every moment. If you are at hand, I would soon be cured of my obsession."

Sofia was surprised at the strong pull to place her hand in his. He would not sell her. He wanted to do a good deed. He was as taken with thoughts of her as she was of him. The thought of receiving charity in any form would have once insulted her, but today, she gravitated to his generosity. Sofia pulled back mentally. She needed to keep her freedom, and a servant in anyone's home would take that away. No, she would have to decline, and that realization made her heart sad.

Sofie reluctantly stood up. "I am sorry, Your Grace, but I cannot sacrifice so much for your tempting offer of restoration of a kind. Good day to you, Sir."

The Duke's other hand came out quickly as he brought the extended one around to grab her arm but not hard. It didn't hurt. "Are you sure, Fia? I want to help you. And me as well. As I said, being with you is a kind of entertainment and an obsession to me. I enjoy your company. Won't you agree? A hot bath and a warm, clean bed in a home defended by plenty of servants and me would allow you restorative sleep."

"Yes," she said longingly, "it would. Good day, Sir. I do thank you for the lovely pastries. They are a weakness of mine."

Trenton let her go because he could see how sad it made her to choose to stay in her squalid conditions. He feared for her in this place. Trenton wanted to see her as a little sister, but he could not. She was delicate and sensitive as well as feisty and sassy. No, his body absolutely did not view her as a relative but a tasty morsel, much like the sweet danishes he watched Fia devour.

How to convince her to come with him before something terrible happened was now foremost on his mind as he returned home to dress for a soiree his heart was not into. Possibly his friends would attend tonight. Trenton needed to speak to them about the avenues available to entice her to come with him. He wanted to bring her home so badly that he was entertaining kidnapping her. No one in that area would stop him, but that would alienate her, which would almost be worse than leaving her. And it would tarnish his integrity which was vital to him. No, there was another way, and he would find it.

Chapter 5

Sofia wanted to cry. She hated the state of her life. She was just on the cusp of coming out into society after the mourning period of her father's death when her life changed forever. To be tossed out into the cold, very literally, was shocking. She had wanted to dance at parties and search out her future husband among the candidates.

Oh, she would never have caught the eye of a man like the Duke, but she had never aspired to that position. Unlike many young women of her age, Sofia wanted security, a home, children, and an indulgent husband. One's prominent position in life was a luxury and a nuisance. The responsibility that came with being a duchess was not to be borne. She was a Lady, but in truth, now she was no one. Her heritage meant nothing if she had nothing to shore it up with. Lords and ladies were plentiful, and missish girls looking to marry would not withhold their charms.

Those with dowries were sought for their societal and monetary assets. The Duke of Trenton did not ask her for anything but companionship for a time. Would being in his company be that bad? The man had crawled under her skin and had taken up residence. It was annoying and wonderful. As she went to find food and something she could safely drink, Sofia couldn't stop herself from listening for his silky deep voice calling out to her.

Her dreams were haunted by him, and when she was dreaming of the Duke, she actually slept. That was a godsend and dangerous. She didn't know what to do to rid herself of him because she knew, in her deepest heart, she didn't want to lose that connection. He would become bored with her soon, and then she would be as she was now, or worse. She would have to take a husband at some point soon if she remained here.

The thought of being with another who drudged just to get through the day was frightening. That evening, knowing her Duke was probably at a fancy party brought tears that fell silently down her cheeks. Her imagination envisioned him dancing, laughing, enjoying the company as he stood, accepting the admiring glances and rude ogling of the women who wanted to be his bride. Women that he would contemplate based on their displayed merits and background.

Her belly ached, and her insides grew that odd queasy feeling at the thought of being with the Duke as his own love. Oh, she didn't love him but to quote her own mother, she was of a certain age to dream, and she fell asleep only to add her new thoughts and feelings to new dreams of the gallant, masterful Devil Duke.

***

Today, after a somewhat restful night, given her circumstances, Sofia was in a good mood. She found water and took the several scraps of discarded flannel she had found in the back of the modiste early one morning and had fashioned them into small bathing cloths. She went to the secluded puddle of rainwater she had found that no one else had found, and she took a refreshing drink before dipping her flannel in.

She wiped herself down the best she could with the addition of a chunk of soap she'd found in the bins out by one of the fancy hotels one dawn. The soap wasn't anything like fancy French-milled, but it did the job. She used the precious slab to help clean her hair and dress when it was raining. Sofia had only done that twice because it took a long time to dry, leaving her wretchedly cold.

She returned to where she had been with the Duke the day before. It was approximately the same time as yesterday. The afternoon stretched on without a sign of the Duke. Disheartened and second-guessing her choice of yesterday, Sofia began to walk away.

"Am I such a bore that you would walk away the moment I arrive?"

Trenton had watched her droop her shoulders as she started to walk away. Good. She must want to go with him, but he wasn't above a bit of bribing to make that happen. It lightened his heart when she turned to face him with an expression of joy. He wanted that look to greet him every time he returned home.

As though she realized there was too much bounce in her step, Fia's face transformed her expression to one of haughty indifference. "I was merely passing and did not expect you. I don't believe you are out on a stroll, Your Grace. The promenade is in the other direction."

"Thank God. I have had enough of that place, but it was naughty of you to mention it." The fact that she had begun to address him properly did not escape him, but he longed to hear his name on her lips.

Fia laughed. "Indeed, I can imagine the horrific strain on your sensibilities to be the catch of the last two, nay three seasons and not want to be caught."

"Yes, that is it entirely." Trenton sat on the rock wall. "It isn't that I don't appreciate beauty, I do, and it isn't that I don't enjoy being fawned over in adoration, but there is a limit, and I fear I have reached it before finding my match."

Fia sat as well. "Surely you can have any available woman. It is a matter of simply choosing."

"Yes, well, there are certain attributes, shall I say, that I enjoy, and those are difficult to find."

Fia frowned. "Such as?"

Trenton suddenly remembered who he was speaking to and what he was about to say. "You are much too young to hear such things." She was insulted. He could tell by the stiffening in her posture. "Look, I have brought you—"

Her tone had turned cold as it had when speaking to his stockman. "I do not care for your trite bits of sweets. I don't care to spend any more time with you. If you will excuse me. And don't return to look for me. I don't need you or your charity."

Fia stood as though she were a child about to flounce out of her mother's sitting room in a huff. Her feelings were hurt. Trenton had forgotten himself and spoke to her as an equal, a male equal. Regardless of her interpretation of that, he would not share those kinds of conversations with a young lady unless she was more than an acquaintance. It was his fault entirely that now she might forego the treat he had brought. And his chance to take her home may have slipped through his fingers. He could not allow that to happen.

"It's marzipan." He reached in his pocket and pulled out the cute little animals made of sweet paste wrapped in a handkerchief.

She hesitated. "Marzipan? I haven't had that in ages. How did you know? I shouldn't."

He began to refold the cloth. "I understand. You are upset that I insulted your age. I apologize, but if you are positive, I will go." He stood as though he had accepted her decision. He turned back. "And you are sure I am unwelcome?"

A delicate hand touched his coat sleeve. "Wait."

"Yes?"

"I might have been too harsh, and you did apologize so well. I could give you another chance."

"Oh, I wouldn't want you to compromise your principles. It has been entertaining getting to know you. I am sorry to have to part ways so soon. I have another engagement, so I should go anyway,"

As he prepared to replace the marzipan in his pocket, he waited for her to apologize and allow him to give her the treats he had brought, but the little she-cat stole them from his hand and took off running. Realizing he couldn't let her go without retrieving her and her apology, he struck out after her. She was stopped by a group of men standing in a narrowed pathway. The men would not move enough for her to wiggle through before Trenton had her in his grasp.

He hauled her to a corner where there was a large, neatly laid stack of bricks. Making sure they were situated so her plump bum would not be seen by others as she kicked the way he knew she would, he began slapping her backside with hard, fast smacks.

"Unhand me, you cad. You bounder!"

Her screeches grew louder as he continued to land the flat of his hand over her dress on the rounded spheres of her bottom. The noisy girl and the punishing Lord were obviously entertaining to the group of men. They had moved to the far side of the buildings to watch. Trenton could hear rude words and laughing, but thankfully, his naughty young Lady couldn't hear anything over her own shouts of outrage. He became outraged that they would say such things about his young lady. He questioned the wisdom of chastising her at that time, but Trenton was always one to deal with things swiftly if possible, and he was nearly done.

Suddenly, just as he had decided he had shown Fia who was in charge and what was acceptable behavior, an incredible pain ripped through the back of his thigh and reached straight to the back of his eyes.

"Ahhh!"

The shock sent him to his feet and the little wretch to the ground. Once he had recovered from the initial shock of pain, he grabbed at Fia and missed, but she dropped her prized marzipan. Stopping to scoop them up was her mistake.

Trenton grabbed her arm and pulled her back to him. She made a terrible sound as though he had wrenched her arm from her body. She was shedding real tears. Had he truly hurt her? Even before he realized she might have been pretending or even more possible, they were the product of his thrashing, he let her go. The second he'd released her—she was gone.

Trenton watched her fly through the alleyway and out the other side before he had decided what to do. He let her go but sent his tiger after her. The young man was well-built and could run. She wouldn't be here tomorrow, of that, he was reasonably confident, but if he could walk after the miscreant bit him hard, he would return. It was important to try one last time. And with the help of his tiger, he'd know where she went.

Climbing into the coach, he could feel the bite outline throb and could almost distinguish her individual teeth impressions without touching the site. He spoke aloud in the carriage. "The damned imp has bested me again. Good thing I go to O'Leary's house tonight. I need reassurances that I know what I'm about." But he knew. He was even more determined than ever. Tomorrow would be the day he brought the feisty woman home with him.

***

"What did you do when the lass took the sweets?" asked the Laird later that evening.

"I spanked her arse. You would have too if you'd seen what she'd done. It was too bad of her, and I had to correct her."

"But in public, Trenton. I'm not sure that was advisable," said Thayer. "For either of you."

"Yes," agreed Ashton, "I'd think it a poor choice. Redden her backside, yes, but in private. You have made her vulnerable to others."

"She did not behave as though her sensibilities are offended. She is a street waif that I have grown fond of regardless of her previous station in life. Because of that, I needed to teach her to treat me better and behave."

Kendrick was quiet until now. "Trenton, it seems as though you are dealing with her as though she would go home and have dinner then go to a social gathering. That isn't the case here. She has some peculiarities that might make you suspect she was once in a decent home, but that was her past. I daresay you can't soften her if she doesn't come with you, and for that to happen, you must show kindness. Think man. She is determined to stay on the streets even though she likely knows what genteel living is. Have you not asked yourself, why?"

Thayer nodded. "I'm afraid he's right. Until she agrees to come with you, training her to be socially acceptable isn't just fruitless; it's cruel. And regardless of the ultimate outcome, treating her as a lady would never go amiss."

Trenton started to pace and then stopped. "Maybe you're right, but I can't tell you how invigorated I am after an encounter with her. My blood is fairly bubbling, and my skin sizzles with the interactions. I can't get the minx out of my head."

"Many good wishes that you can capture her interest and trust enough to bring her in off the streets after today. I'm not sure it can be done," said Thayer.

The Laird offered more whisky to seal his words before they went into dinner. Trenton looked at the wives around the table and thought of his Fia becoming part of the friends' group and how she would enjoy other women in a safer world.

What was he thinking to refer to Fia, even in his mind, as his? He didn't possess her, but he wanted to. No, she would be a great distraction until he was bored with her or found someone to take her place permanently. Yes, he was narrowing his tastes down due to his encounters with the sassy girl. She was helping him, and he would make sure he did right by her. The dilemma was the more he learned from Fia, the less likely it was that any sedate woman would do for him.

The more he thought of it, the better the idea of offering her to his mother as a companion was firming. His mother would not hinder Fia's spiciness or her energy. She would be well cared for, and he could lend a watchful eye. And why did that sound so unsatisfying?

***

Sofia lay in her makeshift bed and wondered if it was time to find a new place to live. Various men had become too attentive to where she went and when she was alone, which was often. And now that she had been seen with the Duke, she imagined they would want whatever he had given her or whatever they perceived she had given him.

Her longings, her hopes and her long-dashed dreams were heightened with the Duke. He highlighted the way she lived now and her losses. Sofia rubbed where he thrashed her, his hand coming in close contact with her actual flesh. He was so close, in fact, that she could feel the heat from his hand that brought on that now familiar tingling between her thighs. It was all-consuming.

"I want to go home with him," she declared to the space around her. "He seems nice if not a bit free with the wielding of his hand to my bum." But it wasn't that simple.

Her resolve was weakening, and that annoyed her. She had caught that big oaf of a guy with the bad teeth and the ruler of the kingdom act hanging around. He had shown some interest in her, and she shivered in repulsion. However, Sofia knew he was just as desperate as she was for some security. Unfortunately, she would have to be even more careful. Being hypervigilant was making her incredibly weary. And the Duke was more enticing every time she encountered him.

No, the time was definitely fast approaching when she needed to leave to find a new place for her own safety, which again led her back to the Duke and his offer. And the realization that if she didn't accept him, it would be the last she ever saw of him. Her chance at a better life would be gone. Would she be a fool to pass it up, even if she forfeited her innocence? She wished she knew.

After yesterday, the fear that he might not return caused her to feel ill. She decided to look for him. As she settled into a spot to sneak a peek at the place she had previously seen the Duke, her arms were held tightly from behind. She was being dragged from the vantage spot, her shoes catching on the debris on the ground, and her shoulders were achingly painful from his tight grasp. She knew it was a man, for a woman was not that large or brawny.

What to do? Sofia screamed. What else, she thought desperately? There was nothing. She couldn't move her arms. She screamed again. He held her too tightly to himself to allow her room to kick him. The animal kept his feet moving enough that she couldn't stomp on his foot. Sofia realized his feet were covered in a heavy boot, making that attempt fruitless.

Realizing she could do nothing else with her body so bound, she screamed a third time. Defending herself, something she had rarely had to do but had become rather good at, was not available to her. Cold fear raced through her veins. She could feel the tremors running through her body, heightening her sensitivity to the man's touch. His putrid breath and the pain and panic were making her dry heave. Nightmarish memories flooded her brain. The workhouse. The same stench.

No one would come to her aid. They were too afraid to do something that would put them in the eye of the attacker. She screamed a fourth time. A big, dirty beefy hand clamped over her nose and mouth. She opened her mouth to scream again, only instead, she bit down on his hand, hard. Sofia held on tenaciously for as long as she could, willing her body not to retch.

An awful metallic taste permeated her mouth, and mixed with the rancid odor in her nostrils, it was overwhelmingly disgusting. Then suddenly, the brute let go. Yanking his hand from her clamped-down jaw that was frozen in place from fear, Sofia could finally breathe, and yet, her chest was still constricted in fear. It hurt to inhale. She caught a glimpse of her attacker. The watchman at the workhouse? No, it couldn't be. And yet it all fit. His lurid looks in the workhouse and sidling up to her before someone hollered at him to leave her alone all flooded back.

Suddenly, Sofia saw his huge fist come down over her, blocking the sun as it slammed against the side of her head. The brute shoved her vibrating head hard against the stone wall, but her shoulder stopped her head from hitting the stone too hard. But the fist had done the real damage, causing the edges of her sight to darken. Her head swam, nausea threatened to overtake her. She instinctively knew she was going to pass out. Footsteps grew further away from her.

By sheer determination, Sofia told herself she was not going to faint. Could not lose consciousness. She staggered and stumbled away from the place the monster had dragged her to. Her next scream stuck in her throat as she tried to stop from throwing up. She could hear shoed horses' hooves coming closer. The clatter of the iron clopping on cobblestone, a distinctively loud sound, was getting closer.

Still trying to control her gagging and the ringing in her ears, Sofia didn't lift her head when she limped to a safer spot. Horses whinnied and squealed, then someone was grabbing her again, and she couldn't fight them. The tears began to roll down her face. It was over.

"Please…" she begged.

"By all that is holy, what happened to you?" The thunderous yet familiar voice was frightening and oddly comforting at the same time. Her Duke.

"A man from the… um… a man." Sofia felt herself being lifted into strong arms. "How would a Duke get such muscles?" Her inner thoughts were inadvertently spoken aloud. Her relief was physical.

"You're hurt, sweetheart. You aren't making much sense, love. Let me get you to the coach, and I'll take you home. My housekeeper will fix you up until I get the doctor." That sounded like heaven.

***

Cragas shoved his throbbing hand in the bucket of rainwater. He almost had her. That girl was going to fetch a good price when he sold her but damn if he didn't want just a sample of her wares first. He would have turned her over, relatively unharmed, but now things were different. He had lost the job at the workhouse when some fucker with money and too soft a heart had him thrown out for "fondling." He'd barely gotten away with his life.

Cragas' luck hadn't been good lately. He'd had to steal women to get his money. Last week, the woman he sold was quickly recognized, and there was hell to pay all the way around. How was Cragas to know that one of the women he had sold after taking his pleasure was the sister to a wealthy estate owner? He'd had to find a new merchant for this particular product because the last one was sitting in Newgate prison.

It had been nearly bloody impossible to get anyone else to trust him after he had supplied the bird of paradise that wasn't. If the Lady ever identified him, he would be hung without a trial by the lady's family. That was why it was a good bit of better luck when he found the girl he'd lost in the workhouse. She slipped out just the night he was going to whisk her away and take her where she worked differently, on her back. He'd watched the girl first thing in the morning for a few days finding her more and more beautiful. His desire to possess her had exceeded any other bit o' fluff. His desires made him overzealous when he decided to take his chances this morning. He wouldn't make that mistake again.

The damnedest thing was, she was a scrappy little fighter, and that was exciting. She was frightened but not enough to forget to fight back. Cragas rather hoped no one bought her when he offered her to the highest bidder so he could keep her, then take what he wanted until she could no longer perform. Then he would toss her off the docks. He had to hurry because that Devil Duke wanted her. He couldn't let that happen.

It would serve her right because he was sure she started his chain of bad luck. He heard others coming, and he didn't want his face seen any more than necessary. He would come back tomorrow morning before she woke up and take her in her sleep. That might work. Use her up and then leave her where she slept. He'd have to think about that.

Chapter 6

The Duke's ire and determination to take care of her was enough to start the tears flowing heavily. Sofia felt herself being set on her feet outside his carriage and guided to the door. She had almost stepped inside when Fia realized he would take her before she was sure she wanted to go. It was tempting, but Sofia wasn't sure if that was what she needed. For the last few months, freedom was access to the open air to go where she wanted. Today the same open-air would keep her stomach from roiling and her brains pounding out of her head.

"Please, Your Grace, I need air. I am still not well."

"Oh, of course." He agreed, but his voice told a different story. He wanted nothing more than to hustle her out of this place, and she wanted to agree.

"Fia, let me take you home where it's safe."

His speech was becoming less formal, and she imagined it was because he genuinely cared what happened to her. They had become friends. If someone like herself could be said to be friends with a duke. They sat in silence. Sofia was leaning against him; he was allowing it. He opened the carriage door and sat her on the floor in the doorway. After some time, she felt better.

Her head still hurt, and her belly was a bit tetchy, but Trenton simply spoke sweetly to her about nothing in particular. He soothed her distress, and Sofia wanted him, his protection and comfort more than she had wanted anything in her life.

After more time for her to feel better, Trenton brought out the honey cake and jar of cider he carried in his pocket.

"I didn't think you were going to come," Sofia said as she gingerly took a bite of the heavenly cake, "So I wasn't going to come this way."

But that was a lie to cover her vulnerability. She had become more adept at that skill since being shoved into the world to find her own way. She was afraid of completely trusting anyone, even the Duke. But today gave her pause. She might trust him to do what was right.

Trenton spoke quietly. "I feared you would not come after you ran away yesterday, but I considered that you might not get many treats like these. I hoped the pull of your appetite would dictate your decision to come."

"Why not the pleasure of your company? Possibly because you thrashed me in public?" her voice told of her hurt feelings and ire over that incident, but her volume was low. Her head hurt considerably.

"Merely a few swats. While you deserved the chastisement, it was insensitive of me to have performed your punishment publicly. I may have unwittingly opened you up to unwanted advances. Like today."

Sofia slowly raised her head to keep it from hurting more. "Did others see my backside?"

"Did others… I did my utmost to keep you hidden from all but my hand."

"And that, Sir, is another thing. You cannot simply use my backside as a place to heat your hand. You have disgraced us both with your indiscretion towards me. I am a young woman." Her tone strengthened slightly, and she winced.

He arched his brow. "Yes, I believe we have established that. But you are also a naughty minx that needs a firm hand. And a Papa to care for you."

"And you intend to be that firm hand?"

"Yes. I intend on being your Papa until you find you do not want one. But be warned, I don't intend on raising a stick, but leather applied to your enticing arse if you are very mischievous is not out of the question."

Her belly was growing warm and tingly in this conversation, and that was not happening. The thought of leaning on a strong, capable man was enticing. She was told all her life that a man like this one was the goal of a woman seeking a suitable man. Wealth, position, power, strength in all areas of life, and if he fancied her, all the better.

But something should be an addendum to that impeccable list, in Sofia's eyes at least, and that was that her husband must allow her autonomy. She might be naïve to want that or even expect it, but her life had irreparably changed this last year. Since she had been on her own, she'd discovered she could handle most things herself. She was not a helpless dimwit as many young ladies were, and she did have some talents from which to draw.

"You're quiet. Did a thought lead you astray?"

Fia shrugged. "Possibly. I am considering your offer, sir."

Trenton stilled. "Excellent. What are your questions?"

"I had not formed any yet, but I shall."

"Do you need anything to bring with you?"

Fia could not tell him that she had nothing to bring, and then she remembered the quilt off her bed, now dirty and worse for the wear. She shrugged instead of speaking. Sofia stared at his treats, only partially eaten. It had been ages since she had something so delectable. It was even better than the jam pastries.

"If you are worried over your virtue, I promise I do not intend to rob you of it." He leaned down and spoke quietly. His voice reverberated deep and dark. "Unless you desire it."

She murmured her response. "As you have previously said. I did not say that was a concern."

But the way her body vibrated at his words, erupting in a wild, almost taboo kind of unnamed urge causing heat to suffuse her body. Sofia instinctively knew it was unseemly.

His finger traced her lips. "It was unnecessary. Your expression tells me more than your lips, little one." Fia shivered and grew warmer and slick between her thighs. Odd. He was just like the devil to make such things happen to her body; things that seemed unnatural.

Sofia remained silent. He was right. She tried to find a way to release that concern, but she had little success based on her earlier predicament. He did appear to be a trustworthy man, though. And isn't a Duke supposed to be a man of impeccable morals? His place in society would mean all would see if he weren't. But did society care about a man's morals? No, not nearly as much as a woman's.

Sofia was not a lady with a knowledge of men and where their whims took them, but she had learned a great many things while scratching out an existence these last couple of months. None of them were things she had ever suspected, but those inevitable lessons had kept her safe and fed thus far until today.

She'd learned never to say yes to any man, no matter how charming and honest he appeared. She longed to say it now to the Duke, but a bite of sweets was not payment for her servitude or her virtue. And yet, they did look and taste so satisfyingly enticing, as did the man who brought them. She savored another taste of the sweet moistness of the cake and the tart bite of the cider. They tasted so good. Pure ambrosia.

That he was an aristocrat showed in his carriage and his conversation. His title of Duke would have had something to do with it. There was a tenderness and cajoling about him that excited her, softened her resolve. Everything about this man had her turned inside out. Could she just stay the afternoon and see if he was truthful? And he had offered a bath of warm water, nay as hot as she wanted it. That would be such luxury indeed.

Just as she was about to put her hand in his, her courage faded. "I'm sorry, Your Grace. I cannot," were her words in parting.

As she ran from that man that was her actual safety net, she felt a hard tug and heard the material of her dress give way. The ominous sound of the fabric as it rent seemed to tear her heart as well.

"Fia, stop," he yelled. Then his voice darkened. "Stop, now!" Her belly tumbled, but she continued to her hiding place. Her tears flowed profusely, and her sight was soon considerably blurred.

His Grace didn't try to follow her for long. She was to a spot she could look at the damage. It was his fault. The Duke's. He'd tried to hold onto her, but she had torn her gown in her haste to run from him. The gown that she had tried so hard to keep as clean as possible. The last bit of her previous life was now in tatters, just as her world was ripped and shorn.

Racing the last distance with her head pounding and her tears streaming, Sofia made sure no one was watching her before she climbed into her hiding place and cried for her day, her sorrow at her losses, and her aloneness. She now had no ties to the world she came from. No longer the coddled darling of her doting parents. Not the annoying little sister her brother always labeled her. She was fooling herself into believing she could retain a piece of her former self. Foolish girl.

    ***

Trenton successfully followed Fia at a distance this time but chose not to disturb her until he had gotten his errands done. He took note of her well-hidden spot but did not want to give it away. Clever girl. Soon enough, he would have her safely under his protection. Trenton left his Tiger to watch over her while he was gone.

She needed to believe she was still safe. Indeed she would be with Trenton's guard watching over her, but he could no longer allow her to stay here. It tore at his belly, and he forced himself to leave her until he had all things ready for receiving her. He understood the need for secrecy to ensure safety, so he turned back the way he came and climbed into his carriage. Johnny, his Tiger, took his post to watch out for Fia until Trenton returned.

He had a final plan that he intended to put into motion immediately. Fia was Trenton's now as sure as if he had bartered for her or announced the banns. He would not abandon what was his. And for the first time since he had met the little bit of sass, he was satisfied where things were going. He was in control, as it should be. And her safety was assured.

Trenton stopped at a well-known modiste in hopes of remedying his earlier mistake. Walking into the shop that his mother often used brought on a strange, out-of-place kind of feeling Trenton wasn't used to experiencing. Since birth, he had been a Viscount and now a duke. These positions always gave him a place in any situation except, it would appear, in a lady's dress shop. Shaking off the need to give this task to another woman, he strode in as though he were expected, and indeed, that good woman did treat him as such.

Trenton didn't want to acknowledge that the modiste had worked with enough aristocratic persons to know how to make them feel important. He simply accepted her offer of personal assistance readily.

"Your Grace, I am surprised to see you in here without your mother."

"I require a gown, rather two, and all the accouterments that go with such a purchase."

"I see, and who is this gown for? Surely not the Dowager Duchess, for I would gladly—"

"No, not my mother, but a young lady who has been caught out without adequate garments due to a… tragedy. She is… unable to come out on her own, so I have offered to help her. An offer I hope you will relieve me of by doing the choosing and assembling without my input."

"I can try, Your Grace. What is the coloring of the young lady?"

"Coloring?"

"Is she fair or dark?"

"Ah, yes, she is fair, with long curling hair, the color of a sable mink and light blue eyes."

"Perfect, and her height?"

He put his hand to his shoulder. "Small… I don't know… no more than that."

"I run into this problem often. Let me show you templates of women, and you tell me which one resembles her best? I have marks on this wall. How tall do you think she is?"

"Ah, that is simple. You have made this much easier than I had hoped."

Trenton picked out the body style he thought best fit Fia and the right height. Within a few moments, the modiste arrived with two beautiful gowns, a beautiful deep blue evening dress he could see Fia in, and the flowing gossamer of the outer layer pleased him.

"It is eye-catching, but do you think she will like it?"

"If you like it, she will love it," replied the dressmaker.

He didn't want to educate her on the fact that Fia didn't base her decisions on his preferences. Quite the contrary, he grimaced. She did the exact opposite, but no longer. He was tired of playing his pipe without her following to his tune. While it was entertaining and refreshing on things that did not matter, when it came to her wellbeing and safety, he would no longer allow her the longitude she presently enjoyed.

"I shall need one more dress and some unmentionables for the lady."

"Yes, this will fit perfectly," said the modiste as she lifted up the second dress she had brought out. "Oh, the beauty of this dress with her coloring will make her stunning, even while doing her household duties. Her dark hair and fair skin will glow." The day dress was indeed beautiful.

Trenton walked out of the Modiste's shop with two gowns and the accouterments when it was all said and done. One dress was blue with silver threads, one green with gold accents, with slippers, combs, brushes, and ribbons for her hair. He simply kept the day dress in the coach. The rest would be in Fia's room when she arrived. Next, he continued home.

"Kerns, a young woman will be returning here with me tonight, but until then, I want her protected, so I have left Johnny there to watch over her."

"I understand, Your Grace." And as the excellent head of staff Kerns was, he never inquired as to why. Trenton could have hired outside his staff for the task, but he couldn't vouch for anyone else's integrity. That was important when dealing with his Fia.

Trenton then sat down with Mrs. Kerns, and together they devised a list of things the lady would need once she arrived at Trenton House. The housekeeper did not inquire about the situation, but unlike her husband, Mrs. Kerns showed her curiosity. All would be clear soon. Now that he had decided as to his next move concerning his young lady, it was easier to make the decisions necessary and delegate the tasks at hand.

"I'll send a footman and my most level-headed maid to acquire the things you need right away, Your Grace. Better a woman does this, Your Grace. We will prepare her room immediately."

"It is as I had hoped, for I am not in the right temper after experiencing the modiste once, to do so again. She was a good lady, and I daresay we will need her again almost immediately, but I will leave the next trip to the young lady and her maid. This little one is sassy and prone to want her own way too often, Mrs. Kern. Please assign a maid that is not taken to whims of fancy, Mrs. Kerns. I couldn't bear two of them colluding to my demise. I will be required to make some decisions at times that will make the young lady irritable. I don't want a maid to further incite her."

"Very wise, Your Grace. I will take care of it. Have you agreed to take a destitute young lady to ward, sir?"

"Why do you ask?"

"Well, most young women have their own gowns, sir. They possess their own toiletries and the like."

"Well interpreted, Mrs. Kerns. Yes, it may come to that, but for now, she will be here under my protection without legal obligations." Trenton nodded. "Very well, I still have business to attend to, so please take care of those and any other issues I have yet to address on her behalf."

"It is done. Is she a special lady, Your Grace?"

"That is what I am trying to determine, Mrs. Kerns. And her name is Fia." Both rose from their chairs.

She nodded. "Now, when will the mite be arriving?" asked Mrs. Kerns as she straightened her skirts about her.

"Tonight."

"And which bedchamber, Your Grace?"

"Put her in the women's suite, if you wouldn't mind."

"But there is an adjoining door to your room, Your Grace." There was a slight hit of reproach.

Trenton heard it and allowed himself a slight grin. Mrs. Kerns treated him as a son, and he enjoyed the relationship. She showed her keen mind often, and Trenton admired her. "Perfect," he said and then waited for Mrs. Kerns to ask what he knew she wanted to.

At first, Mrs. Kerns said nothing. Then, "Do I need to employ a nanny? Because, if so, the nursery is further down—"

"No nanny but listen for a good tutor. I may require one. I may need to ask you to help train Fia on taking care of the home as well. Time will tell. Mother is not coming to the city until the end of the season, if at all, so she will be of no help. I rely on you, Mrs. Kerns, to keep things in order."

"Yes, Your Grace."

Trenton suddenly realized the magnitude of bringing Fia into his home, the responsibility he was taking on and oddly, he was excited at the challenge. Wasn't it Trenton's intention all along to find himself a little one? He hadn't expected her to be so feisty, but that added to the excitement. The adventure. This was right. He knew it down deep in the marrow of his bones.

Now to talk to Thayer about that ward idea. It might have some merit after all because the thought of sending her away after a mere sennight or even fortnight was distasteful. In fact, he could say with all confidence, it would not happen. But she was a beauty and would turn men's heads. As his ward, that could be forestalled.

Luckily, Thayer stopped for a visit and to discuss a business matter with Trenton, saving him the trip.

"You must have been honing your perceptions, Thayer. I was about to take a walk to your end of the street."

"Yes, well, I hadn't been out in two days, so I needed the exercise. Businesses have been rather active, which is one of the reasons for my visit today. The other reason is your young lady. I do not see her or hear her, so she must not have accepted your offer. Tough going." Thayer accepted a seat.

"Yes, well, here it is." Trenton laid out the additions to the story thus far and waited on his friend to reply. Thayer leaned back in his chair and considered his glass of ale.

Thayer spoke with confidence Trenton did not fully possess at this juncture. "I can see she is in need of a papa. She wants to come but doesn't want to make the wrong decision. You can respect that but what you can't do is convince this one with words that it is the right thing. You must prove it. That can only happen if she is here and living the truth of it. So, I absolutely agree with you. You can no longer play games. She has no understanding of the grave situation she is in. Not even one more chance to do what you ask. Take her regardless of her desires."

"Your tune seems to have changed today. You advised me to get Fia's permission on an earlier occasion."

"I did, but Trenton, you obviously have a tendre for the girl. And her safety has been challenged." Thayer leaned forward. "She is young, confused, and it is clear she doesn't know what the best choices for her life are. How can she, not far from her childhood days and obviously left to fend for herself in the lap of hades?" Thayer shook his head vehemently. "No, it is your duty. That is… if it is one you wish to undertake."

Trenton rubbed his sweating palms on his trousers. "It most definitely is what I want."

Thayer nodded. "Then take her home. You cannot continue to frequent the bowels of society without risking your own safety, and it risks hers every time she is seen with you and then left without your protection."

"I hadn't considered that until today. That is why I've dispatched a guard to watch over her until I arrive. Then I will take her with me. It is approaching evening. I had thought to go after this conversation."

"I will leave you then."

"Yes, I agree. I have everything set for Fia's arrival. One more night simply isn't acceptable. I have her protected, but I can't sleep worrying about her."

"Right. You need to take care of business and one little lady."

Their conversation lasted a quarter of an hour more, but Trenton couldn't keep his thoughts off Fia for even that short time. Just a few more hours, little one.

***

Several nights ago, when having dinner with the group of friends he now numbered amongst his closest connections, Lady Ashton made a statement that he disregarded out of hand then, but now it had him worried. Lady Ashton was the wife who had been raised in America and therefore was more outspoken. Ashton said it was the usual reason for her landing over his knee. It also made certain activities more enticing.

"Your Grace, do you not wonder why you are constantly thinking of Fia? I believe it's because you have more feelings for her than you are willing to admit. Rather than wanting to purge her from your mind, you want to chain her to your heart. Begging your pardon, but I think you have deeper feelings than even you know. I could be wrong, but I tend to notice these things."

"Rosemary," said her husband. His chastising tone was meant to curb her tongue.

That good lady smiled sweetly and said, "Lord Ashton is not happy with me, but that might be in my favor tonight."

Trenton watched Ashton's lady walk away, and he smiled. That is what he was looking for and what he saw in Fia. It was also why she haunted him so. Rosemary's words haunted him as well.

The afternoon was waning, and Trenton needed to get back to his Fia. The whole experience sickened him that she was still, stubbornly, in this place and hesitant to trust him but longing to do so. Bringing her a dress and more substantial morsels, this time, a large slice of pork with bread and milk, should help her. He had built trust, and if she resisted, he would take her anyway.

Trenton had resolved that he would have her, and as shrewd a businessman as he was, he believed she was more cunning if the need presented. He imagined she was a missish young lady before this turn of events in her life, but even now, she showed no appreciation for her dangerous lot in life. She was a lamb wandering amongst a pack of wolves. Indeed, she wasn't totally unaware. She couldn't be.

If she weren't so stubborn, he was optimistic his little Fia would have jumped at the chance to come to his home. Well, probably. However, he aimed to fix that and plenty of other things besides. She would learn that listening to her papa was the best move.

Once Trenton had her in his home and under his control, he would change her circumstances for good. The thought of sending her to work outside of his watchful eye sounded less inviting, however. If necessary, he would send her to his mother, and that settled his concerns for her. When he was ready for Fia to go, that was. If he ever did. And only after he was sure that she was secure in that placement. After he purged her from his system. Trenton's inner voice said that would never happen. He was a fool if he thought he would ever let her go. He ignored that inner voice and tried to do the same for his excitement at finally reaching his goal with equal lack of success.

Trenton wore a topcoat over his too fashionable clothing to draw the least attention possible in remembrance of the possible peril that he put himself and Fia in with his presence. He'd done entirely too much of that these last few days already. He took the corked jar of milk he had kept as cold as possible before bringing it with him and the cloth-wrapped food, placing both in his coat pockets.

Trenton had one small sweet in his breast pocket. He would produce it if she came with him without fuss. It was like enticing a child to behave. It was a practice that was ill-advised but often employed.

Treats and gown in hand, Trenton had his driver take him to a street over from where he had discovered Fia stayed. Trenton's Tiger met the carriage.

"She hasn't come out of hiding, but Your Grace, there are plenty of men who frequent the area. Some stop near to where she is. I thought I would have to stand physical guard in front of her, but I guess my size was enough to run all scoundrels off. However, there is one…" Johnny shook his head. "It is just good you are here to fetch her, Your Grace."

Getting out of the carriage, Trenton replaced the gown inside. If he had to chase her, it was better not to have the new dress in the fray.

Fia was like a feral kitten, almost impossible to tame and yet, one didn't want to completely domesticate all the fierceness away in fear of losing the wild beauty that was hers. And like the wild rose, she had a delicate perfection protected by wicked thorns, a poet might say, but a kitten fit her better.

As he approached the little hideaway, he heard a scream and a woman yell, "Help! No!"

That was not some woman. It was his Fia, crying out for help.

Chapter 7

Sofia thought she was dreaming but soon realized this was no dream. She'd cried herself to sleep and had awoken to this. She was being smothered. Something was heavy on her body, something, no *someone*. A big oaf. The rancid clothing and breath gave him away again when she gagged. It was the man from the workhouse. She wouldn't let him get what he wanted from her.

His weight crushed her chest, making the act of breathing painful and labored. Panic was building inside when she found she couldn't move, couldn't scream. His enormous, filthy hand lay heavy over her mouth and nose, making breathing extremely difficult. Fia felt dizzy, light-headed. She gagged. How this miscreant had found her, she had no idea. Was he the same dog face who had tried to grab her earlier? The Duke saved her then, but now there was no one to come to her defense.

Sofia had been meticulous about her coming and goings, but recently, she wasn't as watchful as she should have been, and this was the penalty. Was she to lose her virtue and possibly her life at the hands of a man who would take it violently and without mercy? He moved. It hurt. Sofia screamed and fought like a wild animal, making purchase on his face several times with her dirty and torn nails. She thought about biting him again, and her stomach roiled at the memory of the earlier event. The blood, sweat, and tears mixed with the dirt were nasty, and she was lightheaded with her disgust and fear.

Then a heavy slap to the side of her head sent her reeling. Her head was still tender from his previous attack. It seemed like so many things in her life passed before her mind instantly. She remembered the Duke's man hitting her once and His Grace answering anger over the violence. The Duke. She wished with all her heart she had gone with him. Even if his intentions were to take her virtue, she knew he would have done so with much more care than this beast.

She yelled, kicked, scratched, and sunk her teeth in his flesh with the last remnants of her strength, but it didn't seem to make any difference. He simply became more vicious. Just when Sofia thought she was not to win the fight, the man was gone. The weight was completely and utterly gone.

She could breathe, and even though her small space was infused with the rancid odor of her attacker and the hot putrid scent of his blood, she could take in the air freely. She scrambled to the very back of the little shelter and tried to find something hard with which to hit him again if he returned. She retched in the corner.

Afraid to find out what happened to give her that freedom, Sofia listened intently over her labored breathing, hoping that by some miracle, the scoundrel had given up. But no, she heard fists landing with great force. Her breath was coming a little slower now, allowing her to hear better. Sofia's curiosity drew her from her now violated hiding spot. She could never return here again. She gathered her few possessions worth saving and edged to the entrance of her once safe haven.

Sneaking her head out of her lair, she couldn't believe her eyes. Her dream hero, the Duke himself, was in boxers' stance, just as she had seen her brother and his friends do for fun on the lawn of their home. The Duke was making minced mutton of her intruder. Her relief was physical, and her fear for the Duke should he falter, profound. Another brute of a man stood to the side, and something told her that he was there if her Duke needed help.

When the attacker did not move again but lay moaning on the ground, His Grace took out his handkerchief and wiped the blood from his mouth and knuckles before replacing the used cloth in his pocket. When he looked up at her, there was no cajoling in his expression. No teasing, no gentleness. There was a fierceness of proprietorship and protection. He reached his hand out to her.

"Come. It is not safe here any longer. You have been lucky thus far, but that providence is no longer with you. Come with me. I have brought you a new gown to replace your torn one, and if it is still palatable, food and milk. Come now, take my hand."

He was not requesting. He was demanding her obedience with no expectation of Sofia's refusal. A rush of desire and thrilling anticipation pressed against her chest and put her belly in an uproar. She was mesmerized by his presence.

There was no hesitation this time. "Wait, I have to grab my mother's quilt." He nodded sharply.

Shoving her few meager belongings that she would keep in the folds of the blanket already assembled, Sofia returned. She hastily placed her hand in his and looked back on the ground where the man still did not rise up. The Duke's second stood guard over him. There was movement, however, and she was anxious to leave before he came fully awake again.

Trenton quickly drew her into his cloak and sheltered her from prying eyes. He was so much taller and broader than she that his coat fully enveloped her in its protection beneath his arm. The slight drizzle that was often London's weather was held at bay by this man, the Duke of Trenton's mere presence. He was gentle now. Sofia had been the recipient of his kindness and, on occasion, his condescension due to his upbringing and self-importance, but he was always in control. That's what she needed right now, someone to take the lead until she could hold the reins again.

***

Once inside the carriage, the Duke tapped the roof, and the carriage jerked then moved immediately. As he watched Fia settle in the corner of the embroidered bench seat, he shook his head. Pulling the handkerchief once again from his pocket, Trenton reached for her hands, and when she would pull them away, he gave her a severe frown.

"I have just saved you from a fate no lady should endure, and you would keep your hands from me? I will not have it. Do you hear me? I will not have it. I have catered to you, cajoled, talked, teased, and done all manner of things to encourage you to place your protection in my hands, and when I save you from your fate, you will withhold your hand for cleaning? It will not be tolerated."

Trenton stared as tears rolled down Fia's cheek. Trenton cursed his impatience. He gentled his voice and allowed it to turn naturally to one with a more paternal ring. He hoped she would respond because he was in full Papa mode.

"Come here, little one. I know it is more of a burden than you can carry right now, so allow me to take care of you. I am your protector now." He had never pleaded with anyone in his life, but Trenton knew, at that moment, he would do what it took to gain Fia's trust.

With tears falling faster, Fia sniffled and said, "I'm sorry, Your Grace," she said between the sniffles, "I seem to be unable to stop crying."

His poor waif. She was obviously trying to calm her tears, but they would not subside. Trenton pulled her onto his lap and kissed her wet, gritty cheek. He knew his clothing was becoming incredibly soiled, but he had a valet for a reason. Trenton held Fia until she ceased her tears. He was confused because he had never felt emotion this tender towards a young lady before, and he didn't know how to deal with it. But he did know how to deal with a little one who needed his protection and his care.

Taking his handkerchief and finding a clean square on the cloth, he used her tears to carefully wipe her face the best he could. It was wholly inadequate, but she meekly allowed him to minister to her needs. He was satisfied they had crossed the most significant hurdle thus far, her beginning trust. Fia would need to have a nice hot bath with lots of soap and several water changes to feel clean again, and he intended on providing that and more.

"Are you sufficiently better to have a bite to eat, my dear?" his tone still tender.

"Did you bring me cakes?" her question was hopeful in a weak voice with tearful hiccups interrupting her words.

Had he heard her right? It sounded like Fia was asking for comfort and cakes as she would have with someone she trusted. Someone she could let down her guard with, in a tone that insinuated she had every expectation of being pampered. He took heart in that thought. Her manner was predominately the same, except she had hidden her tiger claws. He would nurture that trusting side to encourage her reliance on him when things were too much. Making her vulnerable would be the first step in meeting Trenton's own desires, but Fia needed her own power back while not carrying the burden. His voice was indulgent but firm.

"Ah, but young ladies are not only to eat cake but other food as well. I did bring you a small treat, but I brought you a more substantial fair first. You are my responsibility now, and while there will be plenty of cakes, there will be other things as well. I have fig and pork with bread and milk."

Trenton sat Fia to the side of him and retrieved the food from his pocket. The bread had crumbled slightly, but the figs and pork were undisturbed. They were in a small bowl, wrapped tightly in cloth and tied with string. Once settled, the Duke handed her a clean blanket which she wrapped around herself and snuggled down into the warmth of it. Her own blanket was in desperate need of a wash and airing.

"You remembered that I was in your wool because of the warmth."

"Yes, I remember. I also remember you are due a hot bottom for your trouble."

Was that a scrunched-up brow? He wasn't sure. But her next statement confirmed his thoughts.

"Not fair, Your Grace. Why would you punish me for crawling in out of the weather? Besides, you said if I come with you, all would be forgotten."

A hearty laugh that was seldom heard from Trenton erupted at her statement. "After much bandying about on your part and work on mine, you mean." He put his hand up in defeat. "Alright. But there will be no more instances where you are not getting the punishment you deserve."

"That will be perfectly acceptable, for I am always a good girl." That statement was given as his sister would have said it when she was a child. Trenton missed Anais, now living in the north of England with her husband, but Fia was not his sister, nor did he have sisterly feelings when thinking of her. Far from it.

"We shall see."

"Oh, indeed we shall," replied a much more collected and confident Fia.

He missed her openly vulnerable self but enjoyed her bravado used to hide her fear. Trenton would do his best to sit back and wait on her to open herself up to him when she was ready. After all, she did come with him today.

***

Sofia tried to eat the food carefully, but being dainty was not possible under these conditions. Trenton watched as she tried to keep her soiled, ripped dress and dirty self in one small spot as though being extra careful to not stain the upholstery, but blast the coach seat. The Duke did not seem to mind, but that could change. He reached out and placed a hand over hers.

"Fia, I care not whether the upholstery is soiled. You have not had a chance to bathe and put on your new gown. This has no value next to you and your safety."

She nodded, but she was somewhat confused. The Duke had shown himself to be kind, gentle, and understanding at times, and exacting, demanding and firm on others. How would she be able to keep up with such mood shifts?

And why was he so kind to her now? Was it because he had what he wanted, or was he genuinely concerned about her welfare? It hardly seemed to make sense, but he drew out her needy side. The side of her that sought comfort, especially in the last few months, and that she had hidden aggressively from others for her own protection.

Fia learned that after her brother left and her cousin showed no mercy in allowing her to stay in residence, it was a pipe dream to ever expect that protection again. She had grown stiff and prickly to keep people away, keep hurt away and stop herself from wanting a caretaker so much.

Did the Duke understand all of that, or was he taunting her? Did he see her flounder, reaching out to him in the unconscious hope that he would take her under his wing? Did she, in her shameful need, somehow call to him in a way that made His Grace possessive and want to keep her safe? Or maybe he knew more about young ladies than she had thought. Maybe he had a sister? Yes, then it would have been second nature to guard the female. And yet, was that better than his being drawn to protect *her* as a single entity?

He nodded in her direction. "Eat before the bread goes dry." He handed her the jar of milk next. Then he was busy with tucking in the blanket and checking her face. "It will bruise and make your face even more colorful, but I don't see any permanent damage. Did he, um, harm you in any other way?"

Sofia shook her head. "Not of any consequence. The monster did not have the time. Thank you for saving me, Your Grace."

"Fia, you must know that you have become important to me. I don't know why or how, precisely, but keeping you safe and happy is of paramount importance to me." Trenton leaned into Fia and used his stage whisper voice, "Besides, I hadn't boxed with an opponent in some time. The exercise invigorated me. I'm a better fencer."

Trenton winked at Fia, drawing out a giggle causing her to dip her head in confusion and excitement. Fia could feel the heat climb her chest to her neck and face. It was such a forward thing to do, but she supposed dukes didn't worry much about propriety behind closed doors. Besides, did he mean it when he said she was important to him? As though he was claiming the right to be her companion? Her protector? More?

Her woman's place was slick, and she had the familiar tingling between her thighs. She chanced a slight smile before returning to her tasty repast. They slowed to a stop while the driver jumped down to do a household task at one of the shops close by. Fia took that opportunity to set the milk bottle down and recork it. She then tried to bite the meat daintily, but that was not a possibility. She held up the thick slice and bit into it.

"I forgot you would have no silverware. Here, allow me, love."

He laid the meat on the cloth it had been brought in and took out a knife from the little bag inside the coach. Trenton then gingerly cut the meat into bite-sized pieces, careful not to cut the cloth or his finger. He picked up a bite of pork and held it out to her. "Eat."

She did, but not until she thanked him for helping her. The way she had lived recently had nearly pushed out the urge to show her appreciation because rarely had anyone done a kindness out of the goodness of their heart. Her teeth touched his finger, and her lips closed around the tidbit and his finger. Sofia feared his ire at that indiscretion, and his eyes did darken but differently than they would in anger. It made her feel funny again. He watched her chew and offered another piece.

"From here on out, you shall have proper utensils with which to eat your meal, or I shall feed you." He smiled. "And always a proper meal."

"Oh, but this is very proper, Sir. I have rarely eaten this well in months."

"Indeed. When did you take up this changed diet?"

"Since my…" her words stopped, and she shoved a bit of bread in her mouth, suddenly chewing ever so slowly.

She had almost given herself away, and that wouldn't do. Fia would be back at the workhouse or some other equally horrid place if he knew. His Grace would not allow her in his home if he knew what kind of family she had come from. Her brother was not a well-regarded man. She could not risk the Duke would have heard of him or, worse yet, have money owed to him.

Sofia vowed to be more on her guard. But something in the back of her mind told her that if he were willing to take her from the docks, then he wouldn't be put off by her brother and his well-earned, detrimental reputation and yet, she could not take the chance.

Trenton knew there was so much more to the story, for his face held that chastising expression he had given her before when he wasn't happy with her reply or behavior. She was learning about him enough to know when she was walking a tenuous line, and another shiver of trepidation ran through her.

"Fia, I do not like avoidance of the truth nor lying. In my book, they are one and the same."

She finished chewing and took up the milk again, taking a drink. "I understand." But she said not another word. The Duke grunted but didn't follow up on his questioning.

The carriage ride was a treat. It had been a while since Sofia was in a coach, making it like a new adventure and a familiar friend. She had not seen this London area in a while, if ever, but soon she noticed her part of town. Before long, she had passed where she once lived and strained her neck to see it for as long as she was able.

"Familiar part of London, I see." But he did not inquire as to why. She merely nodded.

Tipping up the bottle to take a final drink of milk to wash down the last of the food he fed her, Sofia tried to hide her grimace by commenting into the silence. "Your Grace, I don't believe I care any longer for milk. And it might be because I am older now."

"Possibly, but I lean towards the explanation that you have not had milk for a while. The familiarity of its taste is gone. You will grow accustomed to it again." He was so sure of himself.

"And what if I do not wish to reacquaint myself with its flavor?" Her question came out haughty, and she should be ashamed, but she had been her own keeper for months now.

"Then it will be a decision I shall have to help you change. It is a preferred beverage."

"For children."

"For young ladies who need fattening."

"I am not a calf, Sir."

"No, you most assuredly are not," agreed Trenton as his gaze raked boldly over her body. Sofia felt unclothed.

"Do you drink milk, Sir?"

"Yes, on occasion, but you will learn to like it again. I daresay this milk has gotten too warm to drink. I won't demand you drink warm milk if you do not like it."

"I like warm milk, Sir, with vanilla and spice. But I do not like tepid milk."

"Indeed, I quite agree."

She watched his gaze so similar to her own father's when he looked at her mother. It was an indulgent fondness. What it meant, she was not sure, but her mother had liked it. He nodded in the direction of the dress that had been unceremoniously shoved aside in their haste for a speedily escape.

"And what age are you, precisely?"

Sofia answered without any guise, "One and twenty."

"Oh, my dear, I should warn you that you have already earned your first spanking under my roof, and if you care to add to it, you will stick with that little tale, but if you would like to further save yourself, you will show better sense."

"Sir, I assure you, I am truly one and twenty. I was born in the year of our Lord seventeen hundred and ninety."

"Quite possibly, you are telling the truth. I shan't add to your thrashing, but if I find out that you have not been truthful, it will earn its own discipline event."

"You will not smack my…" Sofia closed her lips quickly.

"Bottom." He supplied. She nodded brusquely.

She could feel the blush again, "Yes. You shall not because I do not permit it."

"I see."

The silence was killing her. "Is that all you have to say?"

"Indeed. For the moment, it is all I need say on the subject."

And now she was worried. Did His Grace mean he would not smack her bottom because she did not consent, or did he refrain from any further discussion because he had not changed his mind? Oh, it was infuriating because now she was in that most precarious position of indecision. She dared not ask for fear that he had agreed he would not smack her bottom and then changed his mind in the discussion she would have initiated. No, better to hope for the best and prepare for the worst.

They turned, changing directions that allowed the sun to shine through the window. "Let me have a look at your face again now that we are more relaxed. Turn toward the light."

"I am quite alright. I have had worse." Her frustration at being in a new environment and her familiar lifestyle disrupted was confusing. Even though she hated how she was living, she had become used to it. This change in fortune with this indulgent Duke, though better, was not making her comfortable. It was fighting with the warm cuddly feeling she'd had earlier, and Fia wanted to scream.

"By whom?"

"What are you asking me? By whom, what?"

"Are you chasing butterflies? Who has hit you that hard before today?"

"Your man, for one. I don't wish to encounter him, Sir."

If one didn't believe the Duke to be serious before, his darkening countenance proved he was now. "No, that was unfortunate, and I did later reprimand him. Not everyone knows how to treat a lady as your experiences today will have taught you."

"No, I had learned that prior to today. The days I spent in Clerkenwell taught me more. I should have moved from my hiding spot when I thought it was time, but then I hoped…" she shrugged.

"Clerkenwell?"

Sofia froze. She had said she'd spent time in that horrible place. Was he about to push her out of his carriage? She kept her head down and trembled as she waited. Evidently, the Duke had no qualms about touching her, for he grabbed her chin firmly but not painfully and lifted her face to his.

"How long were you in that place? Do not lie to me, little girl, for I won't tolerate it. Your eyes to mine."

"Please, I didn't think I had a choice."

"How long?" He didn't appear angry, but what was his emotion?

"Six days."

He took a slow deep breath and let it out. Sofia could feel the tears stream down her face, and before she had a chance to say another word, the Duke of Trenton had pulled her onto his lap and kissed her dry lips. She licked them and watched his eyes dilate.

"And you left intact?"

She scrunched up her face. "Intact? Oh. Yes, I said I was untouched."

He held her close. "Thank goodness. You will never have to worry about that place again. Or anything. I will take care of everything you need."

"Including my torn dress?"

Trenton laughed. "And spankings, naughty girl." He hugged her. "I know you are mourning your gown. I hope my offering is to your liking." He sat her back in her seat.

"How did you know my gown was important to me?" She turned and asked in an accusing tone, "How did you find me? And why did you return today?" Trenton lifted his brow. "Your Grace."

His stare softened as he began to speak. "I followed you to make sure you were safe earlier. Your devastation at the ruining of your gown disturbed me. I realized it had to hold much more importance than a regular gown for a lady who had many. Your appearance at the sound of rending material was a testament to that." He nodded in the direction of the gown. "Take a look at the replacement." He appeared to want to say more but swallowed the words.

For the first time, she examined the exquisite deep blue satin material that negated the need for a chemise or extra undergarment and the outer layer of shimmering gossamer material. It was the most stunning dress she had ever owned save for the one she had on currently, and that was no longer a thing of beauty but of ruins.

"Sir, I cannot accept this. I have no way of repaying you." She looked longingly at the gown once more before setting it back on the coach seat beside her.

"It is my repayment to you. I tore your dress, and I am replacing it. You mustn't refuse the settling of the accounts between us. I owe no man or woman and do not expect to begin now."

Well, when he explained it that way, and his manner was adamant, she would have to take it to assuage his honor. "In that case, I thank you. It is a lovely gesture, and I will be delighted to wear it."

They had crossed over into a much posher part of London. She didn't recognize the area, but she did know that a Duke must live in a grand place. Mayfair, the sign read. Yes, very posh indeed.

"What shall I do at your home?" Fia asked.

"Do? Well, what young ladies do, I suppose. Play music, paint, sew, enjoy conversation with the other young women I intend to introduce you. I believe you will enjoy their company."

"I don't play well, my stitches are not neat, and I have not painted, but I do enjoy indulging in a good gossip."

"There will be no gossiping. And I can employ a tutor to assist you in your other artful endeavors."

"I am not a child."

Trenton sighed. "Fia, we have certainly established that fact. Now, it is important to be proficient in one of these ladies' pursuits, so choose, and I will hire a tutor."

"I do not need one."

"You will have one if you need one. I shall have you show me your proficiency, and I will decide."

"You will not." Her tone appalled even herself.

Trenton leaned close to Sofia. "You will do as you are told, my girl or I will administer your first, real spanking on your bared backside. You may help with the decisions made concerning you if you behave, but you will not refuse me. Do I make myself clear?"

Sofia huffed. "Yes, Your Grace." She crossed her arms over her bosom.

"Good. And you are welcome to call me Trenton when we are alone. In fact, I prefer it."

"Like your sister?"

"Absolutely not like my sister. Anise knows when to obey and when to interject her opinion. You have yet to develop that talent. You have earned one tanning for not answering me, avoiding the subject of your background, and for biting me. Are you attempting to add this conversation to the tally?"

"You are a horrid man."

"I can be. Now, what is your full name? I do not believe it is Fia."

"Do you not?"

"Fia, remember, I have the strap if I need it." Again with the stern tone.

Sofia thought quickly. "Sofia."

"And your surname?" When she said nothing, quick as a flash, she found her belly on his thighs and her dress thrown over her head. Trenton was smacking her arse fast and hard.

"Montclair." He continued. "Montclair, Your Grace!" Still no response. "Trenton, I beg your forgiveness for my hesitation. It is Montclair."

"Papa."

"What?"

"I am punishing you for your naughtiness. You call me Papa."

Sofia sighed, and the smacks began again. "Papa. Please stop!"

He did. Rubbing Sofia's upturned bottom as he sat quietly, raising her temperature in another way. "Papa, please stop."

"What, rubbing your backside? I enjoy this immensely. Your family name is Montclair. I shall have to find more of your family. Are you from London?"

"Yes," He landed a hand that left the distinctive *splat* in the air of the coach as it was followed by another on her bottom. "Sir. Papa. Trenton. Oh, you know who you are!"

That made Trenton laugh. "I suppose I should set you up now. We will return here at a later time. I hope you have told me the truth, young lady," said Trenton as he righted her in the seat beside him.

It was her mother's surname, and it was one of her own middle names, so she was not telling a lie precisely. She didn't think his grace would be happy about any untruths based on his response to her age, which was no Banbury tale. She had turned twenty-one recently. She had yet to look at a diary, but the last one she perused confirmed her proximity to the date.

"I perceive your father was English, but your mother was something else? Sofia is more Italian, I think?"

"Correct. My grandparents were Italian and English. Father took mother there on their honeymoon, and mother fell in love with the Italian way of life. She often added things at home to help her remember what she had experienced. She named me Sofia Angelina. It is rather unique. It means wise."

"I hope your name proves to be a better indicator of your future than your past, my lady. Wise Angel is indeed a name one should strive to achieve, but I would charge you not to be too angelic, for that would be an unfortunate loss for us both. I like your spark."

"Yes, for if I was too angelic, you would not be able to smack my backside, sir."

"Yes, and you wouldn't feel the rush it gives you."

The conversation stalled as both passengers thought of the implications of Trenton's statement.

Sofia felt her indignation at the implications rise within her, and her response came out as such. "I am not typically a ruffian, sir, but as the circumstances presented themselves, I adapted. I can change again. However, as to my response to your barbaric means of expressing your displeasure, let me assure you that I feel nothing other than annoyance."

His look of disbelief flashed across his face once again, but he quickly hid it. "Yes, well, we shall address that fallacy another time. Once again, where are your parents?"

Sofia felt her sadness descend. "They are gone, sir. I am of age and have no need of a nursemaid, but it would have been nice to still have my mother."

"Did they not leave you anything that you could have used to support yourself? What of their home?" Sofia was suspiciously quiet. "You require that and more by the looks of things. What type of parents would do such a thing? Were they of little means?"

She didn't respond. Trenton had had enough. The girl was full of half-truths, and a good spanking would set everything right. Not like the small attention-getters she had previously experienced but a real message. For that, he would need more space.

Chapter 8

The coach was approaching a row of well-appointed townhouses. The Duke must be incredibly wealthy indeed if he could afford such a grand place. He spoke previously of a large estate, so this was his London home. What would it be like to live in such luxury and privilege? Sofia didn't really care about money, but she would like to have enough to be comfortable. It would have been the case for her if Horacio Edward Cloverfield, Baron of Cloven, had cared enough to have provided for her when her brother had not.

It was all water under the bridge now. Sofia watched Trenton step down from the carriage before his footman could assist and remove his coat which he then placed over her shoulders. He carefully wrapped the folds of the protective garment around her again. Even if Trenton were cross with her, he protected her sensibilities. He was honorable. And that act of chivalry softened her heart towards him.

"Wait, Your Grace, I need to… She pulled at his hold on her as she leaned back into the coach. "I have it."

Sofia held the beautiful dress in her hand, and with her body enclosed in the overcoat, Trenton led her inside. She stopped again to turn back for her beloved quilt, but Trenton forestalled her. He spoke to the footman giving instructions that the blanket was to be washed and returned while the other items were to be given to the housekeeper for Lady Sofia.

Turning to Sofia, he said, "My dear, this is your new home."

"Oh, but…"

Trenton did not allow her to say another word but directed her toward the staff that met them in the entryway. Sofia was immediately introduced to Mrs. Kerns as that no-nonsense woman would be Sofia's go-to person. He was also careful that the butler, Mr. Kerns, not remove Trenton's coat from Sofia's shoulders.

"The lady is cold, Kerns. Have a footman light the fire in her room, next to mine." He turned to Mrs. Kerns. "Now, my good woman, I believe Lady Sofia is sufficiently fed for now. She will require tea and biscuits once she is bathed and dressed. I fear she will need her bathwater replaced after her first wash, but it is necessary to help the lady feel more herself again."

"Yes, Your Grace. I have a maid chosen for her. We will take care of the wee lass. Now should I have this gown pressed?" Mrs. Kerns asked as she stared at the crumpled new dress.

"Excellent. I was strictly instructed not to put heat on the top material. And what about milady's shoes and the rest?"

"Of course, Your Grace. We have it all laid out and ready."

"I am here in front of you," Sofia grumbled, her dissatisfaction and her manner showing her irritation clearly. "You do not need to speak to others as though I am not in the room."

Mrs. Kerns went dead silent. Not at all put off his stride, Trenton continued. "You are quite right. Is there something that I have said that offends you?"

"Well, no, but you were speaking about me as though I were a child and had no opinions."

"And I have apologized. Are we done? May we move on?"

"No, I want to say something." Sofia waited, but there was no response. "I-I want a chocolate instead of tea."

"No, not now, but you may at breakfast."

"But I prefer chocolate. Your Grace, you said I was to have what I wanted if I came with you."

The room fairly rumbled with the implications of her statement. Trenton first sent a quelling look in the direction of the staff, and then he stared down at Sofia, his face not giving away any thought. "Will you leave us alone, Mrs.

Kerns?" His eyes never leaving Sofia's as the housekeeper responded.

***

"I will start those things for the little lady now, Your Grace." Mrs. Kerns dismissed the staff and shooed them from the foyer.

Mrs. Kerns didn't show her thoughts, but she spoke quietly to her husband before going upstairs to the bedroom. "We have been with the Duke for a long time. I believe we understand his likes and dislikes in women."

"Yes, that is true. What of it?"

"I know what finding such a woman means to the Duke. His trouble at finding a little lady he likes and who has the qualities he is looking for has caused him great concern. He may have found her even if he doesn't know it himself. Poor waif, she looked as though she was about to stomp her foot. His Grace will not be happy with that behavior, but he will be happy to address it." Mrs. Kerns held back a smile as her husband merely shook his head. *It was going to get lively around the place, of that, she was sure. And wasn't that grand?*

***

"I'm leaving. I had thought this was a good idea, but I am humiliated with my presentation and the state of what you surround yourself with. It is grander than I am used to."

"More than recent months or ever?"

"Both. You must know, Your Grace, that you live in splendor most people don't even dream of having. I may have been brought up to be a lady, but we were not this wealthy."

"I see. Do you think your behavior is appropriate for a young lady in any environment?"

His manner was aloof and instructive as if she didn't know how to act in public and he would be her teacher. The man was a pompous arse. She made the error of opening her mouth and giving voice to her thoughts. "You are behaving like a pompous arse."

"Sofia." His voice never raised, but the level of chastisement had deepened. "Do you think your behavior is appropriate?"

Her belly was churning wildly, drawing her hand to it in hopes of settling it. She hadn't an answer for the Duke, for the only correct answer was 'no.' Just as she was about to voice an addition to her opinion of his own condescending behavior, she felt like that little girl deep inside. She was ashamed that she had chosen this moment to throw such an opulent gift in his face after this morning's near disaster. She wondered if a man could sound deadly without being deadly. She wasn't sure but adamantly hoped that was the case here.

"I take your silence as a no. That has earned your backside more attention when I take care of your punishment later today. I have work to do while you bathe and get comfortable. I expect no more naughtiness, or I will have to spank you twice." His thunderous expression held no room for disagreement, and so she gave him none.

"Your Grace..."

A maid came around the corner and introduced herself as Trudy, interrupting whatever Sofia was about to say. "I will be your maid, milady."

"Excellent timing. Lady Montclair requires help with her bathing and dressing."

"But..." His look in Sofia's direction dared her to contradict him. A shiver of anticipation raced through her. Her shoulders slouched, then she nodded her acquiesce.

"Yes, Your Grace," said the maid, who appeared to be a few years older than Sofia herself. While the young woman could not have missed the last part of the Duke's interaction with her, there was no acknowledgment of it on her face. She merely followed the proper response with a bobbed courtesy and offered to lead the way.

"Your sensibilities will be much more agreeable after you are clean and redressed milady."

"I wouldn't count on it," she said. Sofia didn't know what had gotten into her, but she was in a blue-blaze temper and being contrary was her natural response.

"I'm not," he replied succinctly as he patted her bottom when the maid turned away.

Before Sofia could think of an adequate answer back to the man who had suddenly grown larger than life, he'd turned on his heel, and that same heel made no sound as Trenton retreated down the long hallway. There was nothing to do but follow the maid. Sofia would leave later, maybe tomorrow.

***

Trenton listened as he made his way down the hall to the library he used as an office. He had a large room for his study in the country and an equally sizeable library, but here at the townhouse, the room, while spacious, must do double duty as there was only one. Trenton preferred the books surrounding him when he conducted business rather than brocade-covered walls and settees, which is what he found in the room designed for an office. He had used it as a receiving room because he needed that more often, and the library was entirely masculine. Now, Sofie could use the receiving room as her sitting room.

It wasn't that he didn't understand Fia's need to be heard, but she had been alone too long to be instantly agreeable to anything with boundaries that were not of her own making. He expected her to push back and was more than sturdy enough to withstand the storms ahead. He had decided. He was keeping this one for himself.

Trenton had worked for several hours and found he needed something to satisfy his stomach to help him through the next few hours until supper. He leaned back and pulled the bell to summon a servant that was never far.

He was reminded to check on Fia's progress in removing outer traces of her recently abandoned lifestyle.

"Can you tell Mrs. Kerns I would like an update on Lady Montclair? And send in tea."

"Yes, Your Grace."

He had long decided to allow Fia to call him Sir, for any sign of respect from that chit's lips was better than none, but she had fallen to calling him Your Grace so she would soon come up to snuff. She had even, under duress, called him Papa. He was determined to show her that freedom came from living a disciplined life. A completely untamed life led to chaos, devastation, and ruin. None of which he would allow. The footman returned.

"Mrs. Kerns said the young lady is having some difficulty and wonders if you might be able to settle her. She assured me that your tea will be made by the time you have attended to your guest."

The Kerns had been with the Trenton household for as long as he could remember. They both stepped into the household leadership role about ten years ago and had run the place ever since. Unlike so many others, Trenton preferred to take his primary staff with him between houses. He never had to reset his household or remind the staff of his requirements. His central staff did that.

When he was gone, the Kerns had an excellent understaff that stayed in the house they were not living in, keeping things running in his absence. His tiger and coachman were quite adept at ensuring the comfort of the coach and safeguarding Trenton's welfare. He would redirect the staff to put Sofia's concerns first, even above his own. Jimmy was a young, stout man with a powerful body and a noticeable punch. Trenton would make sure that he kept Jimmy attending the carriages that carried Sofia, and when going back to Trenton Hall in Sussex, Jimmy would sit in front with the driver.

Making long-term plans with Sofia sounded right to Trenton, and wasn't that contrary to his first thoughts on this adventure? His hope had been to wash her from his system. However, he was caught in the web Sofia had no idea she had woven. It had been set directly in his pathway. He needed to think about this change in direction, but he would find out why his girl was making such a fuss right now.

His lady needed to answer for her naughtiness. Her accounts were long overdue. His hand had been itching for quite a while, ever since that first encounter, and each encounter since only pointed him in this direction, and now, full relief was in sight. He smiled as he took the steps two at a time, telling himself it was necessary to quickly attend to his girl. It was not because he was eager to see her again, he assured himself.

He wanted to smack her bottom but had no desire to give her any worry or discomfort other than that. He held his step on the first landing and walked up the next few steps with dignity. He heard a screech coming from Sofia's bedroom. Propriety be damned. He leapt up the last few stairs and strode with purpose to her door and, without preamble, threw it open to a sight he'd never thought to see.

The maid was holding out an unbelievably tiny corset. Sofia was on one side of the dressing room with her arms akimbo and her legs ready to take its owner far away. Her hair was dry but wild. Her bosom under her chemise was heaving. He surmised his girl did not want to wear the corset. He thought it was no longer a requirement. Besides, she did have a lovely body, which he could see without any corset to define or confine her curves.

"What the blue devil is going on here?" Trenton allowed his voice to thunder.

Both women stopped and turned to look, shocked, at the Duke.

"Your Grace, you can't, I mean, it isn't seemly. A gentleman never looks upon a lady… unless, well… it's just not done."

"Yes, I understand you, Trudy, but this is an extraordinary case, surely." Trudy didn't appear to agree with his assessment. However, Trenton did not care. The room was strewn with assorted items, water, suds, and bathing accouterments, as well as a wild woman in the midst.

He turned to address Sofia just in time to see her deep intake of breath, likely to release another bellow. This was not to continue. "Sofia Angelina!" When the Duke thundered, the earth seemed to shake. "Stop this instant, or you shall be staring at the floor and feeling the palm of my hand."

To Sofia's credit, she forestalled her next screech. Her countenance was like a spring storm, beautiful and untamed, and Trenton loved it, but it was not the time or place. His bed was a more appropriate environment. He stopped his thoughts from expounding. "Your Grace, I refuse to wear this. It is too confining."

"Yes, I can well imagine. Trudy, please tell me why you want her ladyship to wear it?"

"Sir, she needs to retrain her figure. This will do it in no time."

"There is nothing wrong with my figure! Your Grace, do you think I need such assistance with my figure that it needs retraining?"

Trenton cleared his throat and wondered how he ended up in this mired affair. "Sofie, I will not stand for this type of behavior. You will speak calmly and with decorum, or I will not hear your argument."

Sofie. Trenton had never called her that, but by her softening, she rather liked it. It was intimate. Familiar. He liked it too. Fia crossed her arms over her ample breast and took several deep breaths, likely to settle her nerves.

"Your Grace, I do not want to have my figure 'retrained,' nor do I care if there is a perfect line under my gown."

Trenton asked, "Do you not, my dear? You must be the only young lady who isn't concerned with a smooth presentation."

"It doesn't matter as much as free movement. I have always hated corsets. I cannot breathe, nor can I sit comfortably. It is not a necessity for your household, is it Your Grace? For if it is…"

"It is not." When Sofia opened her mouth after his pronouncement, he made another. "Stop right there. The next words out of your mouth had better include a sincere apology to Trudy. She was charged to make you feel more like yourself. She has tried to do that. You will appreciate her efforts even if you disagree with her choices. You will also apologize for your unladylike behavior, which we will be addressing."

As he stood, his countenance unrelenting, he watched Sofia give up the fight. He doubted she had given it all up, but for now, she relinquished her position. It would suffice.

"Your Grace is right," she said in a subdued tone. "I am truly sorry for making your job harder. I know tending to a woman such as I have become is not your chosen task, and I appreciate that you have undertaken it. I do feel incredibly better after the bath."

"Thank you, milady, and I do enjoy tending to you. I merely wanted to give you what you have lost, a sense of yourself, your pride, milady."

Sofia nodded, and then dejected, she dropped to the cold hard floor and, without any preamble, sobbed. His lady appeared defeated, and that would never do. He scooped his little one off the floor and sat her on the bed.

"Throw the damned corset away. Keep it yourself if you like. It doesn't matter. We won't need it. Where are her brush and her dress? Her slippers?"

Trudy raced to gather all the items she had in various places while Sofia cried. The maid stood with a slight tremble before the Duke and waited for him to continue his instructions.

"Lay them here on your mistress's bed, and I will assist her."

The maid's eyes widened at his scandalous declaration. "Your Grace. It cannot be done."

"Is this my house?"

The maid trembled but held her ground. "Yes, Your Grace."

"Is this my guest?"

The woman nodded and then pleaded with him. "But her reputation, Your Grace—"

"Will not be harmed unless you decide to tell all and sundry, in which case, you will be out on your ear. I think you are well compensated for being an employee in my house and trained to not cross me. If you want to stay in my good graces, understand now that I am a fair and honest man, but I am the master of what is mine. It is, as I say it is, within the walls of my home. Sofia is mine. Take care you do not challenge me again."

Trudy was trembling in earnest now. Mrs. Kerns hustled in the door, all business. She didn't spare the Duke one look but gathered the frightened maid and led her out of the room. She whispered in her ear, and the girl scurried away.

"Your Grace, I am not impressed that you have decided to make your stand at the moment the maid was correct in pointing out the young lady's reputation. You may be lord and master, but I am the one who keeps the order below stairs. Now, I chose her because I thought Lady Montclair would need someone who knew the way of things in this house and society and could correctly guide her. I will leave the matter at your discretion, but I will not have my girls bullied. So, do I dress the young lady, or shall you?"

From the corner of the room came a wavering voice. "I have dressed myself, thank you. I simply need my slippers in Your Grace's hand and my hairbrush."

The two who were engaged in a battle over Sofia looked to see she was indeed dressed. "Well, isn't that a good lass? I'll be sending up the tea tray for both of you. It will take a bit of time to put your hair to rights, my dear. I have a secret weapon that I will send up with your tea. A wild boar bristle brush and start at the bottom. You will be amazed how that will put you to rights in no time."

Mrs. Kerns left the room and closed the door quietly. The air grew heavy with the silence as Trenton put his hand out to Sofia. She accepted the offer and allowed him to lead her to the fireplace. He placed her on the sofa and looked at her tear-streaked face, brushing her untamed locks out of the way.

"You are truly the Devil Duke, Your Grace. I thought I knew where you got your name, but I was wrong. You are wildly devilish, Your Grace, and I swear that flames shot from your eyes. Did you grow a tail?" Her question asked so sweetly and with a tang of mischievousness.

Trenton smiled wearily. "I would not be surprised. It has been a day, hasn't it? It was too bad of me to treat the poor girl in such a manner after having taken you to task for the same thing."

"Maybe you need to apologize as well. You will feel better."

The Duke smiled. "Did it make you feel better?"

"Not really, but I did feel sorry for her. Trudy must learn to stand up for herself. It's the only way anyone will respect her. On the docks, she wouldn't survive."

"Sofie, you don't need to survive any longer. Let me take care of you until you are ready to do things on your own. Safely. This has been a difficult day, and I am sorry."

"I have had longer and harder days." She tried to be off handed about the trying day, but he didn't allow it.

"In some ways, I believe that, but in others, this one has rocked your senses. You have been attacked, assaulted, uprooted, and turned upside down. I could do nothing to make things better today, but we can take it easier from henceforth. Hmm?"

She nodded and sighed. "Yes. I don't know why I feel so vulnerable. I feel all wrong inside, moody, full of unrest. I'm angry with everyone and myself for something so inconsequential as being unable to brush my hair. I'm hungry but don't dare ask for anything because it feels so imposing. I want to snuggle in the bed, I want your approval, and in the same breath, I could stomp off into the street."

"All will be better tomorrow. I do promise you that. There are a few things that we must settle, though, my little grumpy Fia. It will clear the air and allow us to go forward." There was a knock at the door. "Enter."

The tea came, and it was piled high with meats and cheese, bread and butter and jam, and a full pot of tea. "I added a couple of cakes for the wee one. Your little lady looks as though she needs a special tidbit or two."

Trenton smiled at his too perceptive housekeeper. "Thank you, Mrs. Kerns. I am sure Lady Sofia appreciates the kindness. Don't you, my dear?"

Sofia had to drag her attention from the food before her. She was famished. "Yes, I am grateful for your offering. It is a feast."

"I also sent some cold milk for the lass. She might cool her tea with it."

"Excellent forethought. Thank you. Did you bring that special brush for my lady's hopelessly tangled hair?"

Mrs. Kerns pulled a brush from her apron pocket and handed it to her employer. She smiled at Sofia, who smiled shyly back, transforming her face into that of an angel's.

He was going to be hard-pressed to keep his hands to himself. After the door was shut behind Mrs. Kerns, Trenton began to butter the bread and put meat and cheeses as well as a few pickled beets on her plate.

"I don't like those," Fia said, pointing to the beets.

"You haven't tried them, Fia."

"I have. They look like blood. I don't want them."

"However, you will try them, and that is that."

"I am an adult, sir, and if I don't wish to eat them, I will not eat them." She put the beets back into the little bowl.

"This is not up for discussion. You need them. Beets build the blood, so Mrs. Kerns keeps telling me. Fia, you will either try them, or I will spank your rounded arse and take away the cakes."

"You are so ungentlemanly. I have done all you asked today, and now you would punish me for not liking a particular food? Mean spirited—"

"That is all out of your mouth. You will hold your tongue and have your tea. I need some peace, and you need to eat." Sofia's look said she had plenty to say. "Abide by my words, young lady or suffer the consequences."

The Devil Duke was back, and while she would never admit it to a soul, her center was tingling again, and she was releasing fluid between her thighs. It wasn't her monthly because she had just finished it. It had happened each time she'd been in the Duke's presence. Would she leak through her gown?

"What's wrong?"

Drat, did nothing miss his attention? "N-nothing is wrong, Your Grace. I will be fine."

He set the plate of food in front of her, including the horrid beets and milk glass. He poured her tea and allowed her to put her own honey in it. Then he reached for the milk, and she stayed his hand with hers.

"I am now grown. I do not need milk in my tea."

His brow went up. "No? It is quite strong."

"I shall survive, Your Grace." He merely nodded and poured his own cup, then made his own plate of delectable tidbits.

"Take a bite of beets, Fia."

"What if I get sick?" She sat back in her seat and crossed her arms.

He raised his brow. "You won't."

"But what if I do. It will be your fault for forcing a woman to eat horrid things."

"Eat it first." His voice delivered the verdict matter of factly, "and if you are ill, you won't have lost all your tea."

***

Sofia huffed her irritation and shoved a beet into her mouth. The Duke was not easy to deal with as he did not intend to argue any of her well-worded discussion points. How was she to win if he would not debate? He said not a word when Sofia finished the beets, which she found she quite liked. They were in a rather sour and sweet juice like a sweet pickle. He was a kind man to keep his gloating to himself.

When she had eaten enough to stave off her hunger, she reached for her tea and took a drink. The tea was indeed dark and fragrant. And bitter without milk. She tried to find a way to drink it without showing her distaste, but her grimace gave her away. She couldn't add milk now, but she didn't know how she would drink it without the milk.

"Pour in the milk, Fia."

"But…"

"Listen, my dear, I know that you are having a hard time giving over to me, and I can understand to a point, but if one finds the tea too strong, it is customary to add milk to make it better. Your taste doesn't run to strong tea. You require milk."

She frowned. "But you drink it without milk."

He nodded. "I find I rather like it this way. It is certainly not to everyone's taste."

Fia said nothing, but she poured the milk. She sighed her appreciation for the taste after that. It was hard to let go and let him take care of her, even if it were only minor things. She did feel more vulnerable when he spoke to her in such a firm yet caring way. And protected. Valued.

"Sofia, I promise it will get better as you settle into this life. But unless you have any thoughts of leaving without my permission, I would think again. You are mine to care for, and I refuse to let you go for some time, if ever."

After her months of hiding, deprived of even a little luxury, she was desperate to indulge and yet afraid to do so. She wasn't doing a great job of showing how well she could do on her own. Sofia was glad he didn't allow her to do the first foolish thing she had said. She would stay and see what he had for her.

"Your Grace, I appreciate all you have done for me, but I truly don't think I can go back to living a useless life. Please, I just need a way to earn my keep without being at the world's beck and call. I need to feel part of life again, not living on the fringes."

"I'm afraid there is little that I can do for you in that way, my dear. I agree to help you find a good position to put your talents to use when the time is right, but I'm sure you know that we all answer to someone. I answer to my responsibilities that encompass my estate, this townhouse, my businesses, and my partners. The people of my village depend upon me to build a symbiotic relationship with them. To help them meet their responsibilities towards me and my house, their families, and the community. I serve at the pleasure of the King in the House of Lords."

"Ah, but I am a lady and do not need to carry such weight. I may do as I please, and I would please to help in some way. I am not particularly inclined to take a husband, but I will want to help run his house if I do."

"I know a few young ladies who thought the same at one time. Some sentiments have changed, but some have remained the same. I assure you we shall try your talents out in the future, but you may not always do as you like. You will serve at the pleasure of your husband or, in this case, the master of the house. Who does not care a whit if you dawdle your days away or help whoever is in need? You may not, however, throw any further tantrums as I witnessed today. I expect you to *act* the lady even if you do not want to *be* a lady."

She sighed. "I should go. I cannot live this life."

"And yet you are obligated to stay until I am agreeable. You do not know what 'this' life is unless you give it a chance. You accepted my offer to come with me, and I expect a minimum of two weeks, likely longer. It will take a bit of time to build up your wardrobe and find you a genteel position. Surely you can give me that much time."

"I want no spanking."

"Ah, yes, and now we get to the crux of the matter. Your desire to get out of the punishment you have tried so hard to earn. I propose we talk, have our tea, discuss the things that will happen going forward and agree on the punishment you have earned."

"Fine, but no smacking my bottom, for I have had quite enough of that as a child. And very recently, there has been a certain duke who has taken immense pleasure in performing that erroneously perceived duty."

Trenton smiled at Sofia. "I am sure you quite deserved every smack and punishment received, no matter who administered it."

Fia smiled and shrugged. "Possibly. I just didn't seem to find a way to stay out of trouble." She dropped the whimsical tilt of her lips. "However, I am not a child any longer, and naughtiness is not something that I indulge in. Therefore, no need for smacking."

"I believe your disobedient tendencies have something to do with your sassy tongue and curious mind, of which you still nurture. Oh, and let's not forget your courage or your bravado. It is quite the perfect recipe for adventure and disaster."

"It has done me well thus far, Your Grace."

"The adventure or disaster?" Trenton wiped his mouth and leaned closer to Sofia. "Let's make a deal. In private, you call me Trenton or Papa, and I will call you Sofie or Fia."

An embarrassed smile came across her face, and even with her hair in tangles, she felt beautiful. Sofia could apologize when she was in the wrong but be a tiger when she didn't believe she was treated fairly. But how to react to this proclamation?

"Papa, like my cousins call their father? One described it to me as calling an English father, daddy? I do like that. It makes me want to cuddle in your arms." Sofia's face turned blood red. "Oh, I mean… no, I can call you, Your Grace, or… Sir."

"But I don't wish it. Remember, you are pandering to my will, and I am the master of this house. Understood?"

"Yes, I understand." It was difficult to breathe normally.

Sofia would never admit the tremor of giddiness that ran through her at the thought of someone being so nurturing towards her. She was not a child and should squash that thought quickly, but a woman who had entirely too little kindness in the last years, she loved the warmth that word brought.

"And when we are entertaining, I believe Lady Montclair is sufficient, but when in a circle of friends, as I will introduce to you tomorrow, you will be Lady Sofia."

"Your Grace, I'm not sure I can be a good guest or hostess. I am not familiar with the people or the household."

"I propose you allow yourself to be treated as a guest but as a relative might treat the home and friends of another relative. Be comfortable and at ease. Be prepared to allow my home to be yours. I work most days at least a few hours, but you will have plenty to entertain you. I have decided to engage a tutor to help you feel comfortable in your role. Would you like to interview the applicants with me?"

"I would prefer not to have anyone teach me anything."

"But you will accept my offer." There was that tone again.

"If I must." Sofia was anything but thrilled at the prospect of having a tutor.

"And will accept cheerfully," he prompted.

Sofia released a great sigh. "Yes, of course, Your Grace."

"Papa."

"Pardon, Papa." It didn't feel as warm and cozy a word after chastisement, she thought.

"Now, sit in front of the fire, it still has some heat in it, and I will brush out your hair."

"Please don't bother yourself, Your... Papa. I will do it. It will prove to be a tedious task."

"It will be relaxing for both of us. Now do as you're told."

"You do like your own way," she observed with a crooked smile.

"Yes, in nearly everything. Do you want to know a secret?" Trenton asked as he settled her at the right angle.

"Yes, please."

He leaned down to speak close to her ear, "I nearly always get it."

Fia giggled and then put her hand over her mouth. "Where did that come from? I never laugh like that. It feels so magical in a way to be here, after... where I was living."

"It is a giggle, sweet girl, and I hope it's because your heart is lighter. See, you are feeling better already."

By the time they had finished with her hair, long, curling tresses of sable brown flowed down her back. Sofia yawned.

"You are a beautiful woman, Sofia. I am going to be the envy of every man, attached or unattached." He leaned down to see her color up, her blush a deep red. He kissed her cheek. Bold, but he had earned the privilege.

"You embarrass me, Your Grace."

"My apologies, my dear. I had no idea you were so easily discomfited." She didn't answer as she tried to stifle another yawn.

"Right, up you go, my girl, you are in desperate need of a nap, and I have other duties."

Before she could protest, for he could see the words forming, he scooped her up and laid her gently on the bed. He arranged her gown to protect her dignity, although he would have enjoyed a little ankle to kiss. He whispered to her.

"Take a nap, and I will have a surprise for you when you are awake. Sleep at least an hour. Then freshen up and come down. Call your maid, if you wish, to help you and bring you down to me." Sofia opened her mouth to answer. "Hush. I want no discussion. You have not had a safe sleep for months."

"In the cotton, I was safe."

The chuckle rolled out of his mouth. "Yes, I suppose that is as close as you have come. You are protected here, little Fia. No one will harm you. I will see Lady Sofia in the library after your nap." Fia smiled and closed her eyes. "Sweet dreams, little one."

All she could do was smile at the gentleness of her Devil Duke as she fell asleep to dream about the man with great power and wealth. In her dream, he ignored the countless beauties vying for his attention to hold her tight in his arms, shielding her from the world. A man she might learn to trust.

Chapter 9

Waking up several hours later, the sky was darkening, and a quiet shuffle in the room startled Sofia into full wakefulness. She lay perfectly still, listening and trying to remember where she was. It took her a full minute to put her thoughts to right. She relaxed and then heard the movement again.

Once she had been turned out to her own devices, Sofia had to learn how to be watchful even in sleep. She had let down her guard in this house, feeling safe and protected. She was too easily lulled into a sense of calm. The Duke did that to her. He was indeed a silver-tongued devil. Determined to surprise the person lurking in her room, Sofia slid slowly out of the furthest side of the bed, landing on the floor as soundlessly as she could.

The movement was in the part of the room that led to her dressing area. She'd never had a dedicated room in which to dress, and it was rather exciting even if it did feel prickly and stuffy. A bit like the boarding school she had lasted a week in. Her mother was so humiliated, but her father said it didn't matter. They were too restrictive for a free-spirited young lady like his Fia.

Finally, she got a good look at the skulker. "Trudy, what are you doing sneaking around my bedchamber?"

"Oh, no, Miss." Trudy's hand went to her chest. "You frightened me. I wasn't doing any such thing. I was told not to wake you, but I needed to get things cleaned up. You will be having dinner in an hour. That isn't much time to help you prepare."

"For dinner? I will wear this and put my slippers on. I can comb my hair and maybe put it up a bit, but that is enough. Pa-, His Grace wouldn't mind."

"Oh, but he is the one who asked me to help you get ready. Your dress needs to be ironed, and it is a day dress, not one for dinner. I can put up your hair after you put on the green gown. It is for the evening."

"Alright, I will make you a deal."

"A deal? But I have to do as His Grace asked. I don't have a choice."

"Yes, but I do. So, I don't think there is much wrong with this gown save a few wrinkles. So, I will let you put up my hair if I can just wear this gown. But nothing too fancy, just pull it up, yes?"

Trudy seemed to consider the compromise. "If you agree to wear a dab of scent and a touch of rouge."

"Very little of both."

By the time forty-five minutes had passed, Sofia was descending the staircase following Trudy to the library. She couldn't believe that it was the same day she had arrived. A mere twelve hours ago, she was fighting for her life, and now, she was elegant and looked the part of a lady. Just the thought of this day was exhausting.

While part of her revolted against dressing because the Duke had asked for it, her secret bits thrilled at the way he noticed her. Something she hadn't experienced often. Sofia was excited to enjoy the creature comforts she had indulged in growing up. She knocked on the library door.

"Come," said the deep resonate voice of the Duke.

Sofia entered cautiously, as though she expected something to be in wait to pounce on her. She scanned the room for invisible danger, which preoccupied her for a second before her eyes met his. He perused her up and down and up again. His smile was warm and inviting after he took a deep breath and let it out.

"You are a delightful beauty, Sofia."

"You do not have to pretend and give false words, Your Grace. I know I am not the belle of the ball, but the dress is beautiful. I believe Trudy did an excellent job on my hair. That is what makes me look nice."

The smile was gone, and he had a frown in its place. "You need to learn to graciously accept a sincere compliment, Sofia. Did you wish for your present now?

Before we move on to your punishment? Otherwise, we can get the unpleasantness out of the way first so we may enjoy our meal."

"No. I don't need a present, and I am not submitting to punishment."

"Ah, that is too bad. I had wanted to give both to you, but I suppose I will only give you your punishment. Do you remember what it was for?"

"I do not consent." She was adamant, and her stiffly held body bore that out.

"I do not ask for consent. You have already done so by coming to my home. You are under my roof, and I am teaching a lesson." He led her to the sofa. "Do you remember running from me when you were found in the cotton?"

"Yes, but that was survival. And your man knocked me to the ground." Her ire rose.

"And I have dealt with him as I will now deal with you."

"Sir, you said I would not be chastised for that. We discussed that earlier, and it was agreed." Her outrage was clear. Trenton dared not smile at the adorable picture she made.

He continued in his now-familiar casual voice. "Ah, yes, for coming in out of the rain. I did give you that concession. What about the avoidance of answering me truthfully when I asked about your family, your past?" She said nothing. "No response? What about the tantrum you threw earlier and the backtalk?" She shrugged in a characteristically childish way.

Her hand was held in his grasp, not painfully but firmly. Her heartbeat quickened, causing her chest to hurt. Hot, she was so hot, and light perspiration broke out on her skin. Her breath was shallow and fast, making her belly dance. The ache in her lower center increased, sending the tingling down between her legs. The Duke was the only man she had truly felt this strong physical response to, and the rogue was going to smack her bum whether she agreed or not. Oh, the gush again.

Why did she feel like a child about to be thrashed for some mischief? She hadn't done anything that anyone attempting to survive would not have done.

"And what else, Fia?"

"I don't know." Why did she feel so mulish?

"Pity. I'll help you lie over my lap, then." He reached for her.

"Please, sir, I did what I had to do."

"You ran from me several times, you bit me, you told half-truths, and threw a full-blown tantrum. None of this is acceptable in my home or from my beautiful Sofia. I will show you just how I deal with naughty misses."

"Please, Your Grace, I don't want to… this is unseemly, sir."

"Papa is acceptable, as we are alone, but I do not intend you to spin your wheels trying to escape the inevitable. If you are naughty, I will reprimand you, and if necessary, take you right over my knee." He followed words with action.

"But I'm not a—"

"Child. I know. However, you are mine to take care of," he paused to settle her wiggling body with a leg against her thighs. Prepare yourself."

"How can I prepare my—ow!"

"Settle in. You have several transgressions to address. This is a lesson in deportment and what I will expect and what I will not accept."

"Can you not simply tell me?" Sofia screeched.

"You need me to recite the lesson? So be it. You are not to run and hide from me. Do I make myself clear, Fia?" He landed evenly timed swats that were tolerable if too embarrassing for words. The sting was bearable.

"Yes, but I didn't know who you were."

"Now you do. I shall be exceedingly cross if you run from me again."

His hand never stopped its rhythmic smacking over the whole of her arse. It was mortifying to have her bottom spanked, but she was even more worried that her wetness would somehow be discovered. He covered every inch of her sitting area. And the surface of her arse was heating quickly, the smacks harder, leaving a sharper streak of pain.

"Sir, how shall I sit at dinner?" she asked in a higher-pitched voice than usual and a little breathless as though she had run a race.

"The same way you would any other night, properly. Now, where was I? Yes, you will not keep secrets from me, and you will not put yourself in danger needlessly. That is an expectation that, if disobeyed, will get you the strap. I am honest with you and will do my best to refrain from unnecessary risks to ensure you aren't left destitute again. You will do the same."

Her tears were falling quickly now. Trenton's words were beginning to fade to the background in the wake of his heavy hand, but she had heard him. He intended to stay in her life. Keep her safe. It seemed like such a long time since Sofia truly could trust another with her welfare.

Her hand wiped across her wet face. Trenton sighed gently and stopped swatting her for a moment.

"Catch your breath, my dear. We have one more issue to address, and then, if you take the rest of this well, it will be done."

"Yes, sir." Her sniffles were interrupted by hiccups.

Trenton was rubbing her bottom and how she wanted him to continue. Sofia was shocked at the strength of her emotions over a man who had hounded her for days. And brought her food, which he did not have to do. In fact, he put himself in great danger returning to her every day this week. She wanted to be angry with him, but how could she when he had been so kind to her.

But the Duke wasn't kind right now. He was horrid and this spanking bordered on cruelty. He continued to rub her bottom, and she continued to grow slippery. Sofia was sure Trenton was waiting to speak to her, and he wanted her to hear his words before returning to heat her backside. It was already like a fire, and every smack increased the swelling and discomfort to nearly unbearable levels.

"Fia, you never, ever disobey me. I told your maid to help you dress, and you wore the same gown as you had on all day. That is unacceptable. I made sure you had another to change into. Why did you not do as I instructed?"

"Because you have friends visiting tomorrow and I will need to have something to wear. I saved the gown for then. It is a sensible thing to do, Your Grace."

An especially aggressive swat landed on her nates, right in the center of those fleshy globes. "Papa."

"Papa, yes, but you cannot say I had an error in judgment."

"I say you must ask my permission if you want to avoid lying over my lap for chastisement."

His hand landed firmly on her upturned bottom, and in a quick flurry of smacks, Trenton had covered her throbbing bottom again, this time taking in the very tops of her thighs, leaving stinging finger lines of disapproval everywhere. Each swat sent stinging heat and tingling through her lower half.

With each spank, her backside got hotter and more painful. With every sharp swat, she felt more excited and slicked her center further. She lifted her bottom with the last few smacks and was mortified when she realized it.

She screeched. "Papa, please, I cannot suffer any more punishment. You must listen to me. I have reached my limit. Please." In truth, it was the embarrassment.

And then the great sobs started, racking her body with the horrid ripping open of the emotional pain she had endured for months. The physical pain he had subjected her to tonight was cathartic and enlightening. His dominance, whether in word or deed, excited her. Her emotional trauma was cleaned and left open to heal.

As Sofia slowed her crying and fought the immense hiccups that came between breaths, Fia found herself leaning against His Grace's broad chest. How she had gotten there, she could only guess. His soothing voice and quietly spoken words were in part explanation, part nonsense, as he rubbed her back, kissed the top of her head, and cuddled her close. She didn't intend to stay, but this felt so good. She couldn't resist lingering a little longer.

"It will be dinner in a moment, my dear. Do you want your present now?"

"You will still give it to me after how horrid I was?" she asked in a shaky whisper.

"Yes, sweetheart. I had intended to give it to you anyway, but you insisted on being naughty, so I needed to get the unpleasantness out of the way."

"I'm so sorry, Your, um... Papa. I did have some good reasons for my behavior."

"Your reasoning may explain behavior in part, but if you are to be the consummate hostess while you are here, you will need to deal with unpleasantness head-on."

"Yes, I promise I will."

"And you will need to learn restraint. I fear you were not well trained as a child if you display these types of responses now."

"I was well trained to take over a home of my own, but just as I was to be presented, my parents, well, did not survive to return last spring."

***

Trenton waited, but when no other words came, instead of pushing her to further disclose, he continued in his thinking. "We have a great many things to discuss over our dinner, so I expect you will need this little gift and the other bit…well, I couldn't resist."

Trenton slid his repentant little one to the sofa and did not completely hide his smile of satisfaction at her compliant behavior now. He walked to the desk in the corner of the room and picked up a paper-wrapped square. He grabbed another larger box. Sitting each down next to her on the sofa, he took up a new seat in the adjacent chair and waved his hand toward the gifts.

"Open the smaller first."

Sofia's eyes lit up, and she smiled broadly. "I am not very demure when opening things. Will you mind?"

"It is your gift, open as you wish."

Sofia tore the paper and ran her hand over a lovely diary with her name neatly and elegantly written on the red and gold leather cover.

"When did you do this? It has my name on it."

"Indeed. My stationer's shop had bound diaries, and I simply had them script on your name."

"Oh, how perfectly lovely. I only wish to have something to enter into its pages."

"You will soon, I have no doubt. Now the other, my dear."

Untying the paper more sedately this time, she removed the colored paper and found a beautiful riding outfit. "Oh, thank you so very much, Papa! I love this. How did you know I could ride?"

"All properly raised young ladies can ride, my dear."

Sofia lifted out a crop and put it down quickly. "I do not use those on my mounts, sir. I have a good hand, and my commands are obeyed without beating the poor animal."

"Ah, good, for this one is for you. Well, for me to address your little sit upon if you find yourself in need of running away again. Keep it with your things so it is handy if I find I must use it."

"Oh, sir, you will not find the occasion to use such an evil implement."

"Indeed. I hope you may be wrong, but it would be nice for you if it were true."

Sofia gave him a suspicious look. "You like to thrash me, Sir. That is too bad of you."

"I like laying my hands on your backside very much, and if I'm right, you like it too. Not the chastisement but the heat that rises and the churning in your middle. I usually make sure my young lady orgasms at least once, but there is no enjoyment right away for punishment. I want the sting to sit with you a bit before I ease the discomfort."

"Sir, I'm afraid I must claim ignorance. What is an "orgasm? I must say, it doesn't sound pleasant."

Trenton opened his mouth, but instead of explaining, he shook his head. "Just a moment, my dear."

Trenton couldn't believe his little lady full of sass was blissfully unaware of the foreplay before congress, and he was equally relieved she was. He would be careful with her, but just a taste would whet her appetite and fire her curiosity about what other wonderful things might await her with him. Trenton hadn't, at first, thought much about Sofia in that way, but she had turned into the little lady he had hoped to find one day. He was very attracted to her and couldn't imagine another more suited for him than Sofie. *One step at a time.*

    ***

Sofia watched His Grace with a wary eye as he strode to the door purposely. Disappearing into the hallway, Sofia wondered what it was that he was going to do. She had no intention of telling him the confusion she experienced with him, nor would she tell him how much angst she experienced when he spanked her. It was unseemly at best, sinful and wanton at the worst. And yet, he seemed completely at ease with the situation. Well, he would be, wouldn't he?

She worried he would think her experienced if she told him about her achiness, and that was the furthest from the truth there was. She could still feel the heat and the ripples and pulses in her center from the chastisement, and she wasn't sure whether that was an incentive to not repeat the transgression or encouragement to repeat the incident. No, she'd better not do so purposely, for she imagined it would not be the only time she crossed swords with his expectations. No, her Duke would not hesitate to heat her backside often, so she should not encourage the event.

There was murmuring in the hall, then the Duke returned, closing, and locking the door behind him firmly. What was he doing? Wasn't it time for dinner? Oh, this did not bode well for her, she feared. He was a man full of contradictions.

"I will show you, quickly."

"Your Grace?"

He hesitated, giving a chastising look and then his face softened. "Sofia, when we are alone, call me papa except for times like this, when I am exploring with you, then I will call you Sofie or Sofia but never Fia. You will call me Trenton."

His smile was brilliant, almost excited. It took Sofia's breath away at how handsome her Duke was. She watched, mesmerized as His Grace-no *Trenton* rolled up his sleeves and positioned her over the arm of the chair he had just vacated. Just seeing his manly forearms was exciting her, but that was wrong. It had to be. She wiggled to stand.

"No, don't fight me, Sofia. It is something good. I shall have to touch you, my girl, but I promise you will enjoy it."

"Sir, you have already touched me, and it was anything but a pleasurable experience." Well, except for the wanton part. Her chest was already tightening, and her heart was beating against her breast. What had she gotten herself into accepting his request to reside with him?

"Trust me?"

That was the crux of the issue, wasn't it? As much as Sofia didn't want to, she did trust the bounder. Something deep inside told her if she weren't careful, her heart would be engaged fruitlessly. She would be bound to him as if he had tied her with rope, and that would be the end of her future happiness, for a duke would never be interested in her.

She had overheard two maids speaking in the hall earlier in the day before he had come to address her lapse in judgment concerning her reception of the clothing choices. They were whispering, but Sofia had excellent hearing.

"His Grace has never brought one of his *women* home before." Obviously, this woman thought it ill-advised, scandalous even that Sofie would be in his home.

"Mrs. Kerns said that Lady Montclair was perfect for the Duke. You don't think she meant permanently, do you?" She had a strong tone of disapproval.

"Maybe. She seems well and good, but I want to reserve my judgment until I know more."

"He has some peculiar habits, I hear."

"Well, they have already broken the rules of propriety several times over. She might only be fit for the Devil himself."

"Ah, so Mrs. Kerns could be right, for he is the Devil Duke, after all."

Mrs. Kerns appeared from somewhere. "Girls, you will not gossip."

"No, Mrs. Kerns," the young women replied in unison.

What did they mean, peculiarities? And how many women had the Duke had? Sofia was not entirely ignorant of men's liaisons, but she could not be considered knowledgeable, either. Is that what they thought she was? His bit of muslin? It bothered her that the household might think that of her when she was only here for a short time, and then she would be off... doing what exactly she had no idea.

Just the thought of not being near Trenton gave her a twinge of fear. Even though Sofia thought the Duke was high-handed, egotistical, and overbearing, she found her security in him. He had proven himself honorable, protective, possessive, and generous. How could one find fault in those qualities?

On the other hand, he was very demanding. He expected his will to be carried out by all and sundry. He saved her from certain destruction and then made her call him papa in private and threatened to thrash her. Indeed he did take his hand to her. He was intent on embarrassing her, yet he took care of her and battled for her, allowing freedoms such as disposing of the corset.

His Grace, Papa, Trenton, it all confused her at a time when she needed to be able to think clearly. And through it all, she truly liked him, and didn't that confuse her all the more?

Trust him, he had asked, and she did. She lay over the arm of the chair and allowed him to position her. He leaned over her, whispering what she could only believe was an act of seduction. Her first real experience of such behavior from a man who knew all too well what he was doing, and she hated that she wanted it. If he were familiar, so would she be.

"Trenton, I am confused." Sofia heard his swift intake of breath as though he had been given a treasured memento.

"You are so beautiful, my sweet Sofie. When we are engaging in intimacy, touching, I welcome your questions. Sofia is formal and proper for my hostess, Sofie is much more appropriate for times such as these, and Fia, for when I need you to call me Papa. Fia is my little lady, and as such, I will give you treats, cuddles, and spankings when necessary."

"It is so complicated."

"You will soon find the comfort in knowing what is expected of you by the name I use. I will also take my cue from you in what name you initiate. It is easy communication of what you are feeling. I like hearing you call me Trenton."

"You shouldn't. It is for spouses."

"And you. Now, Sofie, I must ask you an important question. I need to know your honest age."

"My age? Did I not tell you one and twenty?"

"You did, but I needed to be assured you stuck to the same number. It is important. Now hush while I make you feel extraordinary. Your first orgasm is a monumental rite of passage and is to be done properly. Are you ready, my darling Sofie?"

"I don't know."

"Fair. What shall you say to me if you want me to stop because something is painful or makes you too uncomfortable? That is after you have allowed me a chance to show the good aspects of the experience."

"Why can I not simply tell you to stop?"

"You will soon find out. Now, a word you do not normally use in conversation, please."

"Cotton." A saucy grin appeared when she looked up at him from her bent position.

Trenton smiled and nodded. "Excellent choice. Now call out "cotton" if you find you cannot abide what I am doing when I touch you. I promise to stop when I hear that word, and we will talk about what makes you uncomfortable."

Without further discussion, Trenton raised her dress and laid it almost reverently over her back. He rubbed her plump, soft and likely still pink backside. The cooler air brought attention to her exposure and that Trenton was caressing her bottom.

"Sir…"

"Hush, sweetheart. I'm not hurting you. I'm preparing you." His lips touched her bum, startling her. She whined her confusion. How could this feel good and bad? It was so, so naughty, and yet, the tingles inside were exciting and were incredible.

"Such a good girl. I'm going to move your legs apart, my dear." And as he spoke, he did precisely that. When Sofie resisted, he firmly tapped her bottom cheeks and massaged her arse a little rougher. "Do not be naughty. I'm trying to enhance your education. I don't want to include a thrashing because you were disobedient."

That tone! She gushed and then panicked, but oddly enough, the Duke was prepared for that. "Are you getting wetter between your creamy thighs? Let me check."

She was burning up and antsy. His lips touched her bottom again, and his fingers touched her so very intimately. Sofie moaned.

"No, please, it isn't right." She said half-heartedly.

"Don't you enjoy it?" His tone said he didn't need to hear the answer to know it.

"But it is wrong, Your Grace."

"I asked if you enjoyed it." He rapped her inner thigh with his fingers, allowing the sting to penetrate as he guided her legs to spread further apart, increasing her distressed sounds.

"Yes, no, oh, Your Grace, I don't know."

His finger swiped her channel. "I know. You're enjoying yourself and are aroused. Excellent."

He stopped talking and began to play with her in earnest. His fingers only touched the outer bits of her channel as though to go further would violate her irreparably, and she indeed wondered if it would. But the rest of her secret sanctuary he plundered. He insinuated himself closely behind her and spread her legs even further, causing her concern.

Trenton repositioned her over the arm, raising her arse high in the air and placing her entire private area on display. The embarrassment made her even more excited. His fingers were heavenly. Sofie had one final thought about propriety, and then his movements in her secret, now exposed, place took over her thinking.

She wanted to tell him to stop and yet didn't dare, for he was giving her such enjoyment. Trenton moved away for a second, but the loss of heat panicked her that he would stop. Then he was there again, rubbing her woman's parts with something firm and warm, causing an inner fire to build within her very core. Each touch stoked that flame until it was blazing. The intensity was too much.

"No, I can't take it. Please, sir, stop."

She was beginning to pant with the effort to push back whatever the tidal wave of feelings was becoming. This couldn't be good. It was scary and incredible. Trenton ignored her and continued with what she now knew was his tongue and fingers. The mental image made her tremble as the leaden feeling increased. Her breasts were aching and painfully heavy. It was hard to picture him *there*, and yet…

"Please, Trenton, something is happening. I think I might die," she whispered fearfully, her breath hitching in her chest.

"Ah, you are close, my dear. Good, for we are far too late for our supper, already. Grab the pillow to your face. It will all be over in a few moments."

She obeyed him without thinking, and his finger danced over her sensitive spot incessantly. Then he spanked her arse and lightly bit into her fleshy bum. An explosion of blinding light filled her sight, and her body began seizing in such a way that she was chasing the heavy sparkling feeling. Her muscles cramped and felt like her hand when fisted and opened multiple times. Her arse flexed, and her whole core took on a life of its own. She was gushing and convulsing, and God help her; it was licentious and fantastical. And she wanted to do it again.

When she could hear and think past the pulsing in her body, the sound of Trenton speaking sweetly to her, rubbing her back and drawing down her gown over her behind was comforting. He lifted her up gently and dropped a kiss on her lips, thumbing the tears from below her eyes.

"Your Grace?"

"Trenton, sweetheart. Was that not amazing?"

"Yes, and scary. You have corrupted me, sir." But her tone was not stern. How could it be when he had given her such an incredible experience.

"I suppose I have, but now, my dear, you know what an orgasm is. I stopped at one, but you can have many."

"Sir, are you positive? I can't imagine one would be able to endure many of those in their lifetime."

"Yes, it is a fact. You can have many in a single encounter. We will explore just how many in one evening at another time. I need sustenance."

"I must look a sight."

"A beautiful sight. Now I will help set you to rights, and then we will go and feed your benefactor."

Her benefactor, indeed. She had no doubt that she had sold her soul to the devil himself, and what a sweet perversion to endure.

Chapter 10

Trenton's partners descended on them the next afternoon. "I warned you I wouldn't be able to keep the women from you for long, Trenton," said Lord Ashton.

"I appreciate you waited until day two," said Trenton. "Actually, you have impeccable timing as I have matters to discuss but didn't like to leave Sofia. Let me introduce everyone."

"If you don't mind, Your Grace, we would like to introduce ourselves over our tea. So please, don't bother yourselves with us," Lady Genevieve announced.

Trenton looked at Sofia, and she wondered if he was concerned for her wellbeing or theirs. She gave him a faint smile, as she had seen her mother give her father many times, followed by a slight nod. He must have understood the non-verbal "it will be fine" signal, for he nodded his reply and led the four men out of the room, presumably going to the library to have their drinks and refreshments and to discuss other, more pressing matters than women were interested in.

A stately woman with a warm smile walked further into the sitting room designated as the receiving room and immediately reached her hand out to Sofia.

"I am Lady Thayer, but please, you may call me Annalise." She turned to the other three ladies as they followed behind her, taking seats in the room. Pointing to the darker blonde woman, she said, "This is Lady Rosemary Ashton. This young lady next to her is Lady Cairistine O'Leary. And in the seat next to you is Lady Genevieve Kendrick."

"I am happy to make your acquaintance, ladies. I am Lady Sofia Montclair. Now, if you would not be offended, and on the strength of the men's partnership, may we dispense with the formal address?"

The others smiled and nodded eagerly. "Yes, let's. It is tiring when we plan to be such good friends," said Rosemary.

Obviously, Lady Annalise was the leader of the pack, so to speak. Her second seemed to be the Scottish lass, Lady Cairistine. After that, it was a toss-up whether Lady Genevieve, the obviously quieter lady, was self-assured enough to step in if need be or if Lady Rosemary, the one with an accent she had heard before from America, was the bolder one. Her money was on Rosemary. Lord Ashton seemed more gentle than Lord Kendrick. She wondered if Rosemary remembered her as the disheveled waif near the docks that she paid to run errands. If she did, she had the good grace to say nothing.

Cairistine, who seemed to have no problem speaking her mind, said, "A lady? Then why were you in the street?"

The others murmured their disquiet at her question. Rosemary spoke again. "Cairis, have you lost all your manners in your heathen country? Treat Sofia with some respect. She is special to His Grace."

Sofia's face was as hot as it was when spending time with His Grace exploring intimacies. "N-no, it's alright. Circumstances beyond my control sent me into the street rather than the ballroom as had been previously expected."

Genevieve, who seemed to have a little more decorum but no less curiosity, asked, "And your family?" Rosemary huffed her disapproval of further questioning.

"My parents are dead, and my brother is gone from England. May I offer you more refreshment?"

"I said not to inundate her with your questions. Now she is unsettled." Annalise gave the other women a frown.

Rosemary quickly pointed out including her in Annalise's chastisement was a mistake. "I was not as insensitive as some people. I refuse to take any responsibility. Sofia is a lovely lady."

"Who is in the room with us," reminded Annalise. The women murmured their awkward apologies. "I don't think your Papa's will be happy to know you have embarrassed our dear Sofia."

They had Papas with control over them? Or did they have *Papas,* as Trenton called himself when she was naughty? It was an interesting concept that she daren't mention, no matter how curious she was.

"Please, tell me about yourselves," invited Sofia.

And that is all it took to take the attention off her own situation and onto their lives. She didn't fool Annalise, though, who watched her quietly from the corner. Annalise had a delicacy about her. She looked much like a little China doll Sofia had loved as a child. Blonde-haired, blue-eyed, and twenty, Annalise Thayer, like Sofia's doll, was beautiful. She sparkled when she showed emotion.

Sofie was sure they would be fast friends until she remembered she wasn't staying. That was the end of any hope for finding new friends in these women, except she could stay if Trenton wished her to. It was all so confusing. And those orgasms were quite a luxury she had been allowed to indulge twice since she arrived yesterday.

The women began to share some of their pre-marital stories with Sofie. Rosemary Thayer Ashton was Lord Thayer's cousin whose father had taken her to America to raise her. When he died, she was lucky enough to board the very ship of her cousin's business partner. Cairistine was also on board, transporting children back to England. They became friends of a kind, and Rosemary, at eighteen years old, and Lord Ashton soon fell in love. Rosemary was also blonde but a warmer honey color than Annalise, and her blue eyes had darker depths, like Lord Thayer's. Annalise's were more cornflower.

Cairistine O'Leary was like her name suggested, green-eyed and red-headed, with such a glorious massive amount of lush hair that Sofia wished to touch it. Cairis, as the others called her, was quite the boisterous one even though she was the eldest of the women at nearly five and twenty. According to her companions, she practiced decorum sometimes, but apparently not often with only women in attendance. Her Scottish brogue was less apparent than her husband's but quite pronounced, nonetheless. She carried a brashness that seemed to mimic her husband.

And last but not least, Sofie observed Lady Genevieve Kendrick. She appeared to be the same age as Annalise in her mannerisms, but Sofie found out she was older, three and twenty to be precise. She had been in control of her own life just a short while before her marriage to Lord Kendrick. Due to an unscrupulous relative, she was nearly forced to marry an ancient lecherous man.

When the conversation lagged, Sofia asked about America, and they were chattering again. That is how the men found their women, sometime later. The Laird's booming voice bounced off the walls. "Lasses, it is time that we took our leave."

"Oh, nay," said Cairistine. "Lady Montclair has just relaxed with us."

"Yes," agreed Rosemary. "That is true."

The sudden lack of boisterous conversation made the room ominous in the silence. The women reassembled themselves and rose to stand next to their husbands as though they had displayed such restraint the whole visit. Their goodbyes were a touch sorrowful, and Sofia felt a tinge of regret. She had just begun to soften to them. And she hadn't been able to ask her questions.

Trenton, who must have sensed Sofie's thoughts, asked, "I have a long day of business on Friday. Do you think the ladies could come again and visit? I hesitate to leave Sofia alone for the whole day."

The women immediately turned to their husbands to plead. Thayer, who often took the group leadership role, said, "Annalise will be delighted." The others followed suit, and soon the day's entertainment was secured.

Once the visitors were safely in their carriages, Sofia stood next to Trenton and watched them leave down the long street. He placed his hand low on her back and guided her up the steps.

"Well, what are your impressions?"

"Of the men? Like you, they exude power, and that is frightening. Unlike you, I am unfamiliar with them, so it is still intimidating. The women? I first thought them uncouth and insensitive, then, as they spoke about their lives, I realized they were similar to me as my life had been less than a year ago." She sighed. "I don't think I'll ever be carefree like them again."

"I hope to change that, my dear. Each had difficulties that brought them to the attention of their husbands much in the same way as your situation brought you to mine." He leaned close. "I have something for you. Come with me."

As they climbed the stairs, he opened the door to a room on the other side of her bedchamber. Inside was a beautiful child's room. "I had everything cleaned and made ready for you. I know it isn't what you're used to, but I feel you need a place to drop all your cares."

As Sofia entered the room, she could feel the heaviness inside her lift. Trenton closed the door and sat down in the rocking chair. "Show Papa your new toys."

Sofia was shocked at first, but then she began to melt inside. Sofia was quickly gone, and Fia began to show her face. She grinned at him.

"Your Grace, I love this."

"Good, but is that how my Fia addresses me?"

She hesitated a moment too long, evidently, for Papa grabbed her hand and, without another word, laid half a dozen heavy, sizzling swats to her bottom, making her dance around him. She stomped her foot angrily.

"That was just plain rude. It isn't my fault that you have all these names for yourself, nay both of us. How do I remember them and when?"

"Sofia. Do you need Papa to spank the nastiness out of you?"

She backed away slowly. "Absolutely not, sir. But you must understand how odd this is." She waved her hand to encompass the room and its inhabitants. "It is unseemly for a woman my age to enjoy the pastimes of younger girls."

"I admit it is different but not as odd as you might think. All of those ladies you met today have those same nicknames from their own proper first name. It is a way of life for them. If they are over-worked, over-worried, or taxed to their limit, they all have a place to go to relieve that strain and a Papa to handle the management of their world."

"All the time?"

"No, of course not. They have a lady of the manor, a more formal side, the one they used to come and leave here today. They have a frivolous and sexy side only their closest friends and husbands see. And then they have a little side that they show only to their husbands, but never other men, including each other's husbands. This is between the couples and not to be discussed. I thought it would help, however, if you were to understand the depth of their personalities."

She nodded. "I see. And that is how you want me to be?"

"I want it to be a fun, relaxing part of you. As your papa, I will take all the burdens when you need me to. They are your bits and pieces to pick up when you are ready."

Her look of confusion was almost comical. "But don't you get tired and need a rest?"

"Sofia, my sweet, you must understand that being with you when you aren't obnoxious is relaxing for me. When you are my little lady, my Fia, I even enjoy the sassy mouth within reason. I don't work when I'm with you. I can focus on you and our play, and it gives me a break as well. We will engage in relaxing activities like riding and going for walks, reading, and discussing things. So many options."

She leveled a look of suspicious disbelief. "You would want to spend time with me or simply find ways to chastise me?"

"I fear you misinterpret my motives. Do I like to spank you? Yes. Do you like to receive it? Yes." He frowned. "Do not begin to open that enchantingly cheeky mouth and try to tell me you do not, for I saw the evidence of your arousal."

Sofia's face burned with embarrassment. "Sir, surely that isn't a proper conversation," she declared in a stage whisper.

"No, I'm sure you are correct, but we have not followed conventions since we have met, have we?" Sofia shook her head. "No. And the one event that has put us over into the extremely familiar was that first experience in the library."

She felt the heat grow hotter. "Yes."

"Yes, and you enjoyed it as much as I did. So let's move on to this room. Now, my little Fia, show me what you have to enjoy in this room so full of lace and frills that your papa is itching." He showed her a mock shiver that made her laugh. She loved this new side of Trenton.

He grinned broadly when Fia giggled and rolled her eyes the way she did as a child. How odd that she felt just as light and carefree as a child. Fia cast her gaze back over the room and nearly dove for the grouping of dolls and clothes. She kept up a constant chatter as she reclothed the babies. She showed Trenton every single one, waiting for his appropriate compliment on each doll's attire. He sat back and relaxed, laughing at the antics of Fia and her dolls.

Oh, how she fervently wished this were her forever life as she grinned back. She felt light, carefree and while she couldn't imagine mindlessly playing with dolls as an adult, this was soothing when all in her world had been anything but comforting since that terrible message arrived, changing her world forever.

***

Thursday afternoon, Sofia found herself discontent with the restrictions Trenton had imposed on her. She wanted to do things on her own. She was moody and petulant in a way she had rarely felt like as an adult.

"I need my space, sir, to do as I please," she demanded.

"You will, but I find that if you do too much, like yesterday, you become testy. I am being a good papa and doing what I can to avoid such behavior."

"But I am a full-grown woman, and I demand some freedoms." There was a brief pause, "Your Grace."

They were in the library. "Close the door, my dear."

Sofia automatically did his bidding and then wondered if that was the smartest thing to do, given they were now alone. The servants never entered a room with Trenton in it without knocking first. Well, it was too late now. She threw herself on the settee. It was amazing how comfortable she felt in this home when so little time had passed since arriving.

"Sofie, what is the problem, truthfully?"

"I'm bored and stifled."

"What did you do before you left your home?"

"Played bad pianoforte, knitted under duress, needlework if requested, went for walks, ran the house in the last year, and rode through the park." She looked downcast.

"Ah, yes, well, your new friends will be here all day tomorrow, and I am sure you could get the supplies you needed with them. I would think you to be less likely to find yourself in the suds if you had company." Trenton leaned back in his chair, obviously quite happy with himself.

"I would love that, sir, if I were not without funds to purchase such items." Her tone suggested he was not as intelligent as first thought.

"Of course, you will use my accounts."

"And where are these accounts, Your Grace?" If she had refused outright, she would have found herself facing the floor with her backside catching the breeze and heating under his hand. Sofia had experienced that little dance one too many times this week to not have learned a few things.

"I will leave you a list."

Sofia nodded. "And what am I to do the rest of today?"

"Go into tea with me, and we can discuss it."

That was the most sensible thing she had heard all day. She looped her arm in his and proceeded to the drawing-room where Mrs. Kerns liked to serve afternoon tea. Sofia had taken the chair opposite Trenton at a small round table set up for cards and refreshments.

Trenton asked casually after they had slaked their first, heavy pangs of hunger, "Where did you say your parents are, my dear?"

"Oh, did I not tell you? That was most remiss of me, for it is a sad tale indeed." She knew she sounded too formal, but it suited her mood, and her Duke did nothing more than raise an eyebrow in question. "Father was dispatched to India, you see, to take care of His Majesty's business. Mama went with him, for she couldn't bear to be away from him for so long."

She took a large bite of blackberry jam without the assistance of bread, licking the spoon clean before setting it next to her plate. The equivalent of taking a mouthful of sugar without the assistance of a cup of tea.

Trenton placed his fork down and reached for his napkin. "Stand up and turn around."

"But I am still famished." Her outrage was clearly seen and heard.

"And you shall eat. Stand up and turn around. You need to learn to obey without backchat."

She scraped back her chair, allowing it to scuttle and screech across the floor loudly.

"Now, lean over the chair with your hand on the seat."

"Please, sir, I won't do it again." Fia had learned to placate His Grace.

Trenton stopped to listen. "Won't do what?"

"Whatever it is that I did, of course." Fia knew the moment the words were out of her mouth that it was a foolish thing to say.

Trenton took the wooden utensil with a squared paddle-like end that always sat on the table beside him these days and rapped it on his open palm. When they weren't entertaining, any home meal could be interrupted by this paddle being wielded in his hand, which was why the servants served and then left when the two dined alone.

Fia lifted her skirt, and Trenton landed three resounding smacks on her upturned bottom, causing Fia to release a loud hiss. Her hand went to the stinging spot only to have her upper thighs each receive a swat. She screeched loudly.

"Is that enough to remind you your hands are never to soothe during your discipline and that spoons of jam must be placed on other food before you consume it?"

"Yes, sir." Fia wiggled and bounced.

He landed two more swats to her bottom. "And those to bring to your mind that a lady never scrapes her chair or screeches." Fia tightened her sore, stinging bottom cheeks.

Fia was contrite. "Yes, Papa."

"I should hope so. These manners of yours are atrocious. I should take you to task more, and you will remember more."

"No, sir, I will not forget."

"Good. Turn around and finish your tea." The evil implement was put back in its honorary spot next to Trenton's plate. He picked up his napkin and replaced it, then picked up his discarded fork.

"It has grown cold." Fia tossed her napkin on the table.

"Rubbish, but it might be slightly colder than it would have been if you had not decided to be such a goose and gobble the jam. Next time remember that before you do something you should not do. Your food is no colder than mine, and I find it still edible. You shall see. Now pick up your napkin, or we will have an even colder tea."

She sat sullen and pouty for a few moments, but when Trenton cleared his throat and lifted one brow, she changed demeanor. A part of her enjoyed the play and the attention, but the other part of her, the more intelligent part, was not sure she could handle a steady diet of instruction at the will of her Duke.

***

Fia began to eat as Trenton expected. She was a girl that did not often leave enough for a bird on her plate. He was glad she had a good appetite, but he wondered if experiencing hunger for those months before she had come to him made her fear she would return to such a time of want. No amount of reassurance seemed to lessen her anxiety, so he made sure he always had a tidbit in his pocket if they went out or on his desk throughout the day. His hope was one day, she would lose that trait.

"Please continue about your parents."

"Oh, I thought I had finished. I was interrupted so unexpectantly."

Trenton nearly choked on his food. "Well, expect it again if you do not control that impertinent mouth."

She watched him out of the corner of her eye. He was not angry and shared a slight lifting of his lips to reassure her. "Yes, Papa."

"Now go on. I will be old and gray before this conversation has come to its natural conclusion."

Sofia sat up straight in the chair and shrugged. "What else is there to tell, Your Grace?"

She was back to formality. Sofia was hiding something because that was one of her tells. He wouldn't stop to call her on it as it was likely what she hoped would happen, thereby affording another diversion to take them off track again. "Are they still in India?"

"Where else would they be? I have already told you they are gone. Why do you persist in asking me the same question?"

She took another bite of jam, being very obvious about spreading it on her piece of scone. He needed to have the jam removed for afternoon tea. She was too fond of sweets by half. Trenton would have it replaced by fruit or a bit of raisin and fig.

"That is my question, and I don't appreciate avoidance at finishing the story, Sofia. Where, exactly, are your parents? When shall they return?"

"Did I not say? The disruption to my conversation has scrambled my brain. No, I did say. They are *gone*, Sir."

"Shall I scramble them more because you are prevaricating?"

Sofia replied as she pushed her plate to the center of the table. "I am not, Your Grace. I have nothing to evade. The truth is they went to India one year ago and were pronounced dead and buried eight months ago. Gone."

"My dear child, I am so sorry."

"Yes, well, it was a noble death. Mother died trying to save a child that was being eaten by a tiger. Father died trying to protect mother."

The room was silent. "Sofia Angelina, that is a horrid Banbury tale. Stand up." Trenton slid his chair back to allow her space to lay over his lap.

"But it is not a tale. That is what the missive said that was delivered to us from London."

"Why is it I have not heard of this brave occurrence? Who sent it to you?"

"I did not actually read it, Your Grace. We decided it wasn't in our best interest to make a scene over it. I did not tell anyone, save you."

"And who is 'we?'"

Sofia said, "I do not wish to discuss this matter further, Your Grace. I am through with disclosures and your table game. I believe I have had my fill and wish to retire to my room. I need a nap."

That surprised him. It was unmistakably Sofia's voice and manner. She did not say her protection word, but she certainly did imply it. She was indeed through with the subject, but something didn't ring true. If she would only give him her father's name, for Montclair was not it, of that he was sure, he could find out the particulars himself. His inquiries had produced nothing. It seemed too fantastical to be true. He would have to take what he knew and what he suspected and inquire about the rest.

Trenton wondered if she was telling a tall tale from her own creation or another's. She said 'we,' and he divined that it was not servants that she referred to but a family member of some kind. The next question to spring to mind was what happened to her family estate, and where the hell were these other family members?

Yes, he would put out feelers and see what surfaced. Unless teasing, she was always quite careful to be truthful, even if her arse paid the price, so it was a mystery he would have to find a way to unravel.

"Yes, of course, my dear. I have things that I must still attend to, so I shall see you at dinner." She appeared to disagree, so he firmed his delivery. "There will be no excuse accepted for tardiness or lack of attendance."

Sofia stood in deep contemplation, but whatever she had thought to say or do was decided against. "Until dinner then, Your Grace."

With a fancy flick of her wrist, the napkin was replaced on the table. After taking a final sip of her milk, she left the table with admirable grace. At least she was drinking her milk when pressed. Her exit from the room was stiff and formal, like any good duchess of class because she was indeed raised a lady.

She was lovely. And he had lost at his attempt to learn much more about her this afternoon, and furthermore, he had driven away Sofia's playful side. He already felt the loss of her company and feared it would only grow worse the further he pried into her previous life. He hated that and would need to mitigate the result of his uncovering her past, something she obviously didn't want to share. He would not hurt her if he could avoid it because her pleasure had become too important to him and his own happiness.

Chapter 11

Trenton was gone when Sofia woke mid-morning, taking with him his valet, one footman, plus the coachman. The house didn't have more than twelve live-in servants. Most of them came with Trenton from his country home, so Sofia felt as though the house was empty. She realized how much activity surrounded the Duke as she started her day. She dressed in too much quiet and ate her breakfast completely uninterrupted by chastisements, laughter, or His Grace's intelligent conversation. He always gave his full attention to her when they were having meals, sitting tea, or spending time together. He was truly the best sort of companion, and Sofia missed him already.

She had begun to wish she were staying more than weeks. A whole week had already passed like a bolt of lightning. She found herself desperate to become indispensable to the Duke so she could stay. She considered forcing him to keep her by allowing herself to be compromised until she remembered that ship had sailed. *I could use it against him, and it would work because he is an honorable man.* Sofia slouched slightly in her chair. *But he would despise me as much as I would despise myself, and that wouldn't serve at all.*

Then if she became ill close to the time he wished her gone, Trenton would keep her as she recovered, and caring for Sofia would endear her to the Duke. But that was dishonest, and she wouldn't feel right. She already suffered the guilt about the information she withheld from him already. Besides, if he didn't want her to stay by then, a few more days would not mean anything.

Was he looking for someone to take her off his hands even now? Or was he still looking for a tutor, as he had said when she had first arrived? There were a few applicants, but Sofia had barely seen them enter before she saw the back of them, never to return. She didn't want a minder or a teacher. She wanted Trenton.

Just as Sofia began that long descent into the abyss of lonely despair, Mr. Kerns came into the sitting room to announce Ladies Kendrick, Thayer, Ashton, and O'Leary were here for her ladyship.

"Oh, delightful." Sofie forgot all of her loneliness.

The four women were soon entering the room and speaking over the top of each other. "Sofia, we have come to keep you company. I hear you need to go to the shops."

"How did you know that?" Sofia turned to Rosemary.

Annalise replied. "Because your Duke came by and asked us to make sure you went to the right shops and got things you needed. I hear you had a few more dresses arrive, but they will never be enough."

"How many is enough?" Sofia asked.

"It isn't the number. It's the occasion, my dear. Your Duke said you were to accompany him to the end-of-season party and will need something for that," said Genevieve, who now had lost some of her reticence to join the conversation.

Cairis continued. "And we can help you with accessories, like scents, and rouge and the like. Do you wear a corset?" she asked, taking an assessing look at Sofia's body.

"No, and I won't. Those things are horrid."

"Not ever?" asked Genevieve.

"Never."

"Does the Duke agree?" asked Annalise.

"Yes, we have talked about it, and he agrees I may do as I like."

"You are fortunate. I love your dark hair and eyes with your creamy skin. You will make a beautiful bride. His Grace picked well," said Rosemary.

The room became unnaturally silent. Sofia spoke into that quiet. "Oh, but we aren't marrying. Trenton, I mean the Duke is going to help me find a position."

"That may be what you are telling each other, but we see a different story," announced Genevieve. "That man is enamored of you, and you adore him. It is quite plain to see. So, even if you haven't acknowledged it yourselves, it is nevertheless true. We must dress you as a future duchess."

"Yes, and we should hurry, or we won't be back for tea, and I have been famished lately," declared Cairis. Annalise and Rosemary exchanged a look, but neither responded.

"But shouldn't we have a look at what you do have first?" asked Annalise. She turned to Cairis. "A very quick look, Cairis dear." Cairis nodded.

"Cairis, I have plenty left from my breakfast tray. I ate in here, so please slake your hunger." Cairis took no time to accept the invitation.

After taking a quick inventory of Sofia's clothing and accessories, the ladies gathered themselves and wiggled into Annalise's coach after taking two apples to tide Cairis over until tea. Odd though it was, Sofia watched intently as the coach passed people and shops searching for something. With a jolt, she realized she was searching for a glimpse of the Duke even though she had no idea where he would be. Close on the heels of Genevieve's declaration, it shook her thinking about what her future plans would include. Was Trenton a part of her future or simply a temporary stopover in her present?

Sofia tried hard to attend to what the other women discussed, but it was nearly impossible to keep up with the lightning-fast conversation. These ladies knew each other well, and Sofia was only learning them. Not for the first time, she wished she could call them friends. Acquaintances were all they would ever be, but then, that was better than recent history. She would have to be content.

The shops were bustling as the women, who, en group, could easily fill a modiste's place of business, wove in and out of the establishments with the practiced ease of familiarity.

"Four gowns are quite enough," protested Sofia.

"Not nearly enough, my dear, but the modiste has your measurements. I think if we pick out several beautiful materials and patterns, then those can come later." Rosemary nodded at a particularly bold red. "You can wear two of the ones we picked out today for day dresses. You need to have enough so that you have something else to wear when your soiled dresses must be cleaned. Washing day is but once a week, remember.

"No, His Grace did not mean for me to spend so lavishly. He will be cross."

"Did he not?" asked Cairis. "Then I wonder why he charged us to make sure we purchased what was necessary to make you feel beautiful for all occasions?"

Sofia's eyes widened. "He did no such thing."

Annalise nodded. "He did, and I believe he did so because he feared you would purchase one plain dress and one or two undergarments, and that would have been the sum total. He will be cross if we don't do an adequate job of outfitting what is his. He wants you to feel you are in the same league as any other lady, for indeed you are."

"I was," corrected Sofia. "That no longer is true."

"Oh?" queried Cairis, obviously attempting to garner a strong response. "Did your father lose his position in the world? I mean once a lord…"

"No, but if not for His Grace, no one would have been the wiser where I was living."

"My dear, you carry yourself like a woman who was brought up well," said Annalise. "I was not brought up well, but Lord Thayer told me it did not matter to him. It was my spirit that drew him to me."

Rosemary leaned in closer, "And likely your arse." The women grinned and nodded, making sounds of agreement. All except Sofia, who appeared to be confused.

"But the Duke is not taken with me in the same way."

Her four companions murmured their disagreement as they chose the accessories from several shops. Finally, tired and famished, the women abandoned any further wandering and returned home, much more subdued than when they had set off. Tea and a more sedate conversation were enjoyed before the women took their leave. Still, His Grace had not arrived home.

"We would love to stay, but I fear Lord Kendrick will come for me in a disagreeable mood if I am too much later," announced Genevieve.

"Och, aye. My Laird is the same," said Cairis.

The women bade Sofia a good night as they got back into Annalise's coach and headed home. As soon as her new friends, for she felt she could call them that now, were gone from sight, Sofia felt the loss of their exuberance, leaving her in an irritable mood. She could not go out because of the approaching darkness. Not only was it dangerous for a woman to be out after dark, but it was also not allowed, according to Trenton.

Her treacherous mind had begun to tempt her with fearful thoughts. Maybe Trenton wouldn't return tonight. Or tomorrow. What if he left and returned to his home in the country? No, he would have sent for his servants. Right? The Kerns, anyway. Maybe he had found out the truth and was, at that very moment, finding a way to remove her from his home.

She had no idea what he was doing, but each hour he stayed away, she created more elaborate and injurious thoughts of her inadequacy and his discovery of those insufficiencies. Sofia walked into Trenton's library to the smell of his cheroot permeating the air. Combined with his own distinctive masculine scent, she felt wrapped in his arms of possessive protection. She sat in his chair, imagining his chastisement. Feeling his touch as he taught her about orgasms and kisses.

A terrible thought crossed her mind. Was she just a plaything to her Duke? A woman who, if anyone suspected her experiences with the Duke of Trenton, would be an outcast with no reputation to protect? Had the fiend shown her carnal pleasures only to send her away, possibly to yearn for years for the same intimacy with another? That was cruel, and he wasn't that depraved, was he?

Her imagination was running rampant. No, Trenton simply would help her find a better place in life and nothing else, so she needed to treat this time with him as that, a steppingstone to a better life. Except, there was no better life than the one she was living. Sofia heard the coachman in the entryway looking for Mr. Kerns, and she rushed out of the library in hopes that she would see the Duke and her wild imaginings would end.

"Martindale, where is His Grace?" asked Sofia with trepidation.

"Not here, milady. His business has not concluded, so he will not return tonight. He gave me a note for you and for Mr. Kerns." The coachman handed a piece of folded paper to Sofia.

"Thank you. Are you to return for His Grace tomorrow?"

"No, Lady Montclair. He will take a hack home when he finishes. He does not want you to worry."

"That is ridiculous. If the Duke is in the city, he could have come home." The coachman simply stared at her, prompting Sofia to thank him and leave the entryway.

Sofia carried her note into the sitting room and looked at all the items they had purchased today. Needle, thread, and cloth for embroidery, paint supplies, a new music book, and new reading books for women.

She didn't want it if she was to be sent away. He couldn't even do it himself, so he sent his servant to do it for him. How lame could the man have been? Having his friends' wives help her purchase things to pay her off. It was disgusting and totally against all she believed about Trenton. Flouncing into the chair, she opened the sheet of paper and read:

My Dearest Sofie (notice not Sofia and not Fia),

I apologize for not concluding my affairs in enough time to return tonight. I will try to be finished tomorrow, but something has presented itself that I cannot leave undone. Ensure you eat your dinner and do not stay up late relaxing and playing with your dolls or entertaining yourself with your new activities.

If you are frightened or need comfort, you may ask your maid to sleep in your room, or you may sleep in my bed. Take your fluffy toys to bed with you if you like.

I shall be home soon, and I do not want to hear you have been naughty.

Yours affectionately,
Trenton

She couldn't control her smile as she read the sweet note. Sofia relaxed. Maybe he didn't want to be rid of her after all. He simply had more to do than he had expected. That happens. Sofia's insecurities were now considerably calmer, and she went into dinner. The staff was extra considerate, taking care of all her needs before she voiced them. She went to bed when her maid came to undress her, even though it was more routine than out of necessity. Sofia could and often did dress and undress alone. She and Trenton disagreed on this often, but she took comfort in doing things his way while he was gone.

She was glad that she could sleep in the duke's bed if she needed comfort. It was what Trenton wanted and, therefore, what she would do. But she wasn't upset any longer. Trenton had known just what to do to ease her insecurities. She read for a short while amidst his scent, and the comfortable feeling of his things around her lent a level of security. She cuddled amongst his bedding before nodding off to sleep with a much calmer heart and mind.

The next day, she worked on keeping herself occupied, but the same thoughts of doubt began to creep into her mind, and by early evening, she decided to go out. It irritated her that she had all these destructive thoughts, but she had been betrayed by those she least expected, her family. Why would she believe Trenton to be any different? She gathered her cloak and prepared to leave for a walk.

"But, milady, it is nearing dark."

"There is at least an hour or more before half-light."

"Yes, that is true. It is also true that His Grace would not want you to go out alone. Your maid will go with you."

"I am capable of going for a walk without assistance," she snapped.

"Except that, I have forbidden it," answered the deep voice behind her. Turning swiftly, Sofia did her best to restrain herself from throwing her body into Trenton's arms, but it was to no avail. She sailed into his waiting arms.

"Your Grace, where did you come from? I did not see the coach arrive."

"I had to speak to Lord Thayer, so I walked from there. I needed the fresh air after the last two days in close quarters. Now, might I persuade you to forego your walk until tomorrow in favor of having supper with me in the library?"

"Oh, yes, Your Grace, I would be happy to do so." Fia was battling with Sofie and Sofia, but thankfully, Sofie won out. For now.

He smiled. When the Devil Duke genuinely smiled, his eyes brightened, his countenance transformed to the most handsome of men. And Sofia swooned in her heart as it swelled with glowing love and pride. Love? Did she love him? Maybe not yet, but she was well on her way. That thought brought on all kinds of perplexity, and she was not entertaining any of that tonight.

When Trenton put a hand at the small of her back, as was his habit, an intense sizzle of excitement spread throughout her body. Sofia trembled with the strength of it. Trenton closed the door behind them and led her to a sofa near the fireplace. A fire had been laid, and he lit it, smiling with satisfaction when it took quickly.

Sitting next to Sofie, he asked, "And how are you, my dear?"

"I am well," she replied stiffly. Her hands twisted in her lap, and her tongue came out to lick her lips.

"Well? I had hoped for a more descriptive response than that. What have you done while I was busy away from you?"

And that question opened her Fia door, and out she tumbled. "Oh, well, the ladies and I went to the shops. It was great fun. I have ever so many things." She leaned in to whisper her secret. "I don't know what to do with everything, but hopefully, Trudy does." She sat further back and saw his indulgent smile. "It was not good of you, Papa, to go to Lady Thayer's home and instruct her on what to purchase. It was too much."

"Hmm, was that because you had no issues with spending my money or because you were forced to do so?"

Fia played with the lace on her dress. "Well, we did spend your money. Too much, I'm afraid, sir. They insisted, but I can send it back. Honest. I won't mind."

"My sweet girl, I can afford to keep you in a manner befitting a lady."

"Good, because they are adorable," said Sofie.

Reaching for her hand, Trenton leaned over and kissed her cheek and then her lips ever so gently. "Now, before you tell me all the wonderful things you wasted my money on, I need my supper." He rang the bell, and in a couple of moments, the tray of food was brought in, followed by a tea service.

Trenton leaned back and waved his hand in the direction of the tea tray. Now that her excitement was lessened, it was Sofie who took over the task of pouring and serving His Grace. Funny how she didn't resent waiting on him the few times he allowed it. He had served her more than she had him. After a few moments of eating, Trenton spoke.

"Now, tell me all that you bought." Sofie recounted everything she had, offering to go and get them if necessary.

"If it is too much, I can send them back. It was hard to resist when the others were encouraging me and not allowing me to hold back."

"Excellent. If you send one item back because of cost, I will redden that backside until all you can do is stand. Do you understand me?"

"Truly, you aren't cross?"

His blustering tone diminished to an indulgent one. "Truly, Sofie, I do not mind and am thankful for the ladies doing as I requested. Now, I have something serious to discuss with you. I had thought not to mention it until I had more information, but I think I will be able to get the rest if I have some verification from you."

"Is it serious?"

"Yes, but not a problem." When she nodded, Trenton continued. "Montclair. That name has niggled at my brain for days, and finally, I had some answer to the reason."

"Is that where you went, sir?"

"Partially, yes. Your mother was a Montclair, am I correct?"

"Yes, but I didn't lie," she rushed to explain, "it is part of my name."

"Indeed," he said dryly. "We will discuss that later. What is your full last name, Sofia?"

"Cloverfield."

"Yes, I thought it might be. And you have one sibling named Robert."

"But I did not lie about the fact that circumstances after Robert received the notice of my parents' demise, led me to live as you found me."

Trenton's face was grim and, if she were honest, looked almost angry. "Of that, I have no doubt. Why didn't you tell me that he was the reason you were scratching out a living in that deplorable way?"

Sofia sat straighter and could feel her inner need to protect her family's reputation rise up against the affront of his words regardless of the truth of the reality. "I lived as best I could, sir, and I do not take kindly to you describing it in that way."

"You do not take kindly?" Trent stood forcefully and walked the length of the library twice before speaking. "Sofia, you were not bred to live in those conditions. You were ill-prepared and very nearly assaulted horribly. It was a death sentence to throw you to the wolves, and I won't apologize for being angry at your brother for his unconscionable treatment of you. He was supposed to shield you from the unpleasantness of the city, nay, the world. And yet, he sold all but his birthright and left you to survive the best you could. If I could have him in my grasp, I would strangle him with my bare hands."

Sofia had not heard the Duke speak in such strong terms and with so much venom. She reached her hand to his as he drew close. "But, Trenton, you saved me. I am no longer in such dire straits."

Trenton took a few cleansing breaths while staring out of the French doors a few moments to rein his emotions in before turning to look her in the face. "Yes, and I will never allow you to be alone or without care again."

"I'm not sure what you mean."

"I mean, my dear, that I have become your guardian."

The hope that he would declare himself was crushed. His words destroyed it. "Guardian? Sir, I do not require a guardian. It isn't what I thought…" Sofia shook her head in dismissal.

"You are in need, and I have procured your safety." He stood to open his leather satchel and pulled out duly sealed and signed documents to that effect.

"I don't want a guardian. I need someone who will be with me. I don't need to be added to someone's responsibilities to be checked on periodically as a token of goodwill. I need… to leave." Sofia's despondency was profound, but for once, her needs were entirely missed by Trenton, who was warming to his subject.

"Of course, you don't want one. That's why you need one. You need a guiding hand, and I want there to be no stain on your reputation. Now, I have hired a tutor in the art of finding a suitable husband."

"What?" she asked. Her bemusement did not shift Trenton from his do-good stance. He thought he had done well, but he had broken her heart.

"Evidently, men are not able to understand the complexities of the female gender, or so I have been told. So, I have engaged a woman who can help you understand the ways of women when finding a husband."

"You have… oh, Trenton, don't you understand? I don't need someone who can propel me into society. I need—"

What she needed or wanted was obviously not on His Grace's agenda, for he appeared so enamored with his solution to the problem that he continued speaking, completely ignoring her demeanor or her crestfallen expression. Her horror that Trenton apparently perceived her to require assistance re-entering society drove her to nearly scream her anger and pain.

"Your Grace, may I please be excused?" she broke into one of the few seconds of silence between his animated plans.

"Oh, are you tired, my dear?" Trenton was immediately contrite.

"Yes. I believe the boiled meat did not settle well."

"Oh, then please lie down. We will speak again when you are feeling well."

"Yes."

Except Sofia didn't believe she would ever feel right again. She had begun to realize she was falling in love with Trenton, and to find out he only saw her as a girl who needed a tutor to guide her to find a husband other than himself was more than she could bear. His plans for her hadn't completely changed, as she had hoped, but moved even further in the wrong direction.

She had to leave, but where could she go? Not where she had been just a short time ago. No, that would not do. She would never be able to survive, and she was more educated about the world now. Lady Thayer, that is who she would call on. Tomorrow, she would go visit Annalise. She would be able to help her find someplace to go.

She declined dinner and began to slowly formulate her plan. Sofia undressed before her maid appeared, dismissing her quickly before sobbing herself to sleep.

Chapter 12

Trenton had nearly rescinded his newly executed guardianship paperwork and scooped Sofie up in his arms, taking her straight to bed. He'd wanted to lay his leather and his hands on her after hearing she was contemplating going out alone. Yes, it was safe in Mayfair, but it wasn't the country, and a woman should never go out alone. Ever. And she knew it, hence the leather.

But he had refrained, his decision assisted by the presence of the coachman and his good news. He would never embarrass her on purpose outside of their private times. Trenton had thought Sofia would be happy to be secure in her future, but she looked shocked and devastated if he were honest. He, Thayer, and Kendrick had agreed it would be a good idea to secure her future, but Laird O'Leary and Ashton had a dissenting opinion.

"The lass is looking for *you* to be her security, not some legal jargon." O'Leary had been quite sure of his opinion.

"You are her sanctuary, Trenton. If you do this, do not let her think that it is the only option open to her, or you will find your lady gone." Ashton sounded as though he were speaking from experience. But they didn't know his Sofie.

Trenton shook his head. "No, she has been forced to live on the streets before coming to me. She won't go there willingly."

"Maybe not, but there are many different interpretations of living on the streets, don't forget." Ashton shifted forward in his chair.

"Aye, as a bit o' fluff for one."

"Not that Sofia would contemplate it, but I daresay it would have been her next decision if you had not scooped her out of the situation she lived in."

Ashton was not smiling, nor was he speaking for effect, and Trenton sensed it. But he didn't want to scare

Sofie and had thought this would help her relax. After observing her response to his news, Ashton and O'Leary might have been right after all.

Trenton looked at the message on his desk in the library after Sofie left tea so suddenly. He had lost his appetite as well after seeing her misunderstanding of his motive. He would give her time to sulk, be irritated, and then think through his decision. She was a sensible woman, and she would see that it was protection. Since knowing her, he continuously operated in her best interest, and she would remember that.

Glancing at the note again, he lifted it up and hoped it contained the information he needed. Quickly perusing the words, he sat down and slowly read the note twice more before pouring himself his best scotch whisky.

He would have to leave his girl again, and this time, if it worked out the way he hoped, he would be able to declare a closer affinity with Sofia than he had mentioned previously. The time would be right to share his desires but not before. He'd talk to Thayer and the others, gaining their agreement to watch over her while he was settling this one last bit of business and hopefully procure more of their insight.

His mind drifted to his sassy little lady. She had not had Fia out to play in a few days. He enjoyed the few moments he saw her excited about her new things, but she was gone too quickly. He missed the innocence when his Fia was in the room. Maybe he could tease that out tonight.

But Fia was not to make an appearance this evening. Sofia had sent her regrets to dinner. Trenton had often dined alone without a thought, but now, after sharing meals with Sofia, her absence was sorely missed. She had filled up empty crevices in his life that he had rarely noticed were bare until her personality was fully integrated into his.

Trenton feared he was falling in love with the chit, which was the determining factor for making her his ward.

He needed to distance himself, and propriety would not allow him to cross over the lines he had previously crossed. He had thought he wasn't for her, even if she was exactly what he had wanted. She was still so much of an innocent, and he was anything but one. He'd already corrupted her. If the truth were known, she would have been labeled an outcast, a fallen woman.

The longer Trenton kept her with him, without a solid plan of exit, he ran the risk of deflowering her, ruining her forever. *And loving her completely.* The delicious thought lingered, proclaiming that it was precisely what he should do so she would want, no *have* to marry him. He could make her happy, give her every desire she dreamed of, and she would be his little lady, his mistress, and his hostess. She would be his darling duchess.

His chest swelled at her ability to be all he had ever wanted and yet not lose sight of her own person. It was seen as a character flaw in many social circles, indeed his own exclusive circle, but when she stood up for herself, managed what she could easily do, he knew having a capable woman was infinitely better than a sniveling, foolish one. Sofia thought for herself. It would bring them to cross purposes often enough, but that, too, had its rewards.

Even as he thought it, he knew it was wrong to force her to be something he wanted and not what she desired. Is that what he had done with the guardianship papers? But didn't she enjoy her multifaceted role with him? He saw her relax, smile, become carefree. Those were the reactions of a woman enjoying herself. She still hesitated to call him Trenton to his face, but that would come with time. No, she had misinterpreted, and he had misstepped.

Trenton had given her several orgasms since the first, and at each first touch, she protested. That was a given, but she had never cried her word to stop. She had also given over quicker each time he reached for her. No, his girl craved the lover's touch. His touch. And he did love her.

It was time to admit it to himself that he had claimed her since that first afternoon in his home. Earlier, most likely. Time enough to convince her that she was made for him and he for her. For the moment, the guardianship was his undisputed claim and authority against all comers that would try to get in the way of his plan. He planned on his being the only touch she would ever know. He would soon be teaching her much more than a hand and tongue-initiated orgasm.

The tutor was a bit over the top, but Sofia had said she was bored. Having a tutor would help her do more things to fill her day. Also, in light of the recent letter, his need to be gone had now extended. A tutor would give her a companion. Her maid had other duties when she was not helping Sofia. At Trenton Hall in Sussex, it would be different, but here, the quarters were not as large, so he had only so many servants.

He would have the ladies come over often while he went to find this relative of Sofie's he had discovered. She would be entertained by the women, and Sofia, of course, could go to them. It was a good plan.

The cousin living in her family home in London had not been tough to locate thanks to the brash man's loudly proclaiming he was the new Baron. After Trenton had teased out the full story of her abandonment, his naughty woman would answer for giving him only her partial name and situation, but for now, Trenton would settle her affairs.
***

Sofia hesitated until it was too late to leave the next morning as she had planned the night before. No, His Grace had mentioned at breakfast that he would have to leave for a week, possibly more, and that he was glad the tutor would arrive soon.

"If we are in luck, she will come before I leave, and I will re-acquaint myself with her and establish your routine before I go. If she comes after, I will leave it up to you to do the right thing by this woman. I expect a polished young lady after this endeavor. You will ensure that happens by being obedient."

Sofia looked up and smiled wanly. "Yes, Papa."

"No, not Papa. Your Grace, or Sir. I intend this to be heard loud and clear by Lady Sofia." She sniffed.

"As you wish, Your Grace." Sofia continued to push around her eggs on her plate before finally dropping her silverware to the plate with a loud clatter.

She saw him raise his brow before casting a look in the direction of the footman and maid, who for once had stayed in the dining room. She heard the quiet "snick" of the door closing and took a deep breath. He had sent them away. He was going to chastise her. The beating of her heart increased. Her belly and cunny region quivered in anticipation, and still, she protested.

"I am finished, Your Grace."

"Fia, you are petulant, and it is unacceptable. We do not drop our silverware to announce our irritation. Get into position."

"Your Grace, I…" he didn't cut her off as she had expected. He was waiting for her to finish her thoughts. She had kept her words formal and her tone stiff because it was the only way she would have been able to watch him, hear him, without breaking down and crying. Well fine. If she couldn't be honest now, in the eleventh hour of their time together, then she was useless in creating her own happiness.

"Fia."

And damn him. That tone, that derivative of her name, it took her to the little lady he claimed she was and blast if she didn't want to cry. She raised her eyes to his, looking for understanding. No, she wanted him to stand firm and yet worried if he did.

"Fia, I will not ask you again. If I must mention my request again, you will be spanked long and hard."

Did she want that? Yes. Was she anxious? Yes. But dammit all, she needed that personal connection this gave her. She slowly shook her head and raised it up to stare into his face, deliberately stubborn, tears shimmering. How would he interpret it?

"You said you were speaking to Sofia. I could not be Fia. Now you call me Fia. It is the fickleness that confuses me, and you are the biggest culprit of my confusion."

Trenton held her gaze for a few seconds, his thoughts flitting across his face, and then she saw it. That glimmer of understanding, of softening.

"You need this. Sofie needs this, not Fia. My Fia is secure in who she is with me. My playful, darling, little duchess. Lady Sofia knows her obligations, for she is bound by rules and expectations, but my Sofie, the one I am bound to body and soul on a deep visceral level, is unsure. She is the confused one. Sofie requires this to be confident of her place in my life. Sofie is unsure of my regard."

She didn't answer but lowered her head and stood, turning to leave the room as if to encourage him to continue. His chair scraped back across the wooden floor planks polished to a silken shine. She shivered but took a step toward the door, laying her napkin on the table. He grasped her upper arm firmly. Sofie halted.

"Sofie, promise me this is what you want. That I have interpreted your requirements correctly."

"I make no promises, Sir, for I am not sure, myself. But I will not stop you because I require something. I'm so lost and confused about who I am with you, why I am here. I have to have something to hold on to."

"Good enough," he said as he wiped her tears. "You mean more to me than anyone in the world. *Anyone.* I want what is best for you. I want you."

Leading her back to the table, he laid her over the far end of it. Lifting her so her bottom was on full display and her legs swung in the empty space between tabletop and floor. She wasn't tall enough to stand and lean over entirely. Trenton used that to his advantage at times, but this incident felt more like a formal preparation of a momentous event.

He slowly raised her petticoat and her dress skirt to bare her plump bottom to the room. His warm hand caressed her skin, causing goose flesh to appear as the cooler air, and his ministrations raised the level of sensitivity over her entire body as it reacted to his touch.

Suddenly, he shifted her off the table and strode with her skirt askew through the door and into the hallway, following it to his study and placed her on the sofa. He then locked the door before returning to Sofie, who had not moved from where he had placed her.

Trenton draped her over the back of the settee and displayed her as he had in the dining room, stopping to caress her bared behind, rubbing, and kissing her back and arse while whispering sweet words. Sofie mewed and moaned her arousal. He patted her bottom several times before stepping back from her.

His footfalls were confident as he strode to the cabinet in the corner of the room. Trenton's narrow cupboard was off-limits to the household. He unlocked the door and opened it. Just hearing the key jingle and the lock disengage sent her body into heated anticipation. Hearing the cabinet open but not seeing the contents increased her active imagination, especially as she knew what types of items it held.

The whole mind taunt ratcheted her angst as she was sure Trenton counted on. There were leather implements of all shapes and sizes, wooden punishment instruments, implements for the cunny and arse tools. All of Trenton's favorites were housed inside. Sofie sighed. He had interpreted her correctly.

Sofie heard the door lock, and she inhaled loudly. Once again, warm lips touched her skin, moving from the top of her backside to her fully exposed arse. Trenton laid his wares carefully, strategically within her sight.

"Are you well?" he whispered in her ear, nipping at the lobe, and kissing her exposed neck.

"Y-yes, Sir."

A more significant plug than he had used the first time was lying near her cheek. "Shall I play with your beautiful dark entrance?"

The memory of what had happened one recent afternoon, when Sofie had wanted to go riding, but Trenton refused because it was threatening rain. As compensation, he offered to show her some of his favorite things. Trenton had opened his cabinet then and explained every instrument's use. The one thing he had introduced her to was a backside plug.

Since then, he had suggested more play soon. Today, Sofie could see from the corner of her eye clothespins for her tits, a broad strap and a thinner one. And cloth. And something for her hidden arse entrance. She knew what he would do now. Her cunny cried its anticipated tease of a painful and yet joyful finish.

"Do you say your word?"

She shook her head. "No, sir."

"What is your word, sweet Sofie?"

"Cotton."

"Very well. I intend to plug you, strap you, stretch you and cause your little titties to cry out in a painful ache that will make your cunny overjoyed. Do you wish your word now?"

"No, sir," but her words held a hitch in the delivery.

"I intend to make you cry and beg. Do you wish your word?"

"Please, sir, no."

"You must be more specific, darling. No, don't do it, or no word?"

"No word, Your Grace." Her body fairly trembled, and her honey was leaking down from her core, causing her inner thighs to become wet and sticky as she clenched and relaxed in expectation.

"Very well, but you will say your word if you need to."

Trenton slapped her backside a handful of times before standing her to remove her dress. Next, he returned her to the sofa, fully naked, bending to kiss her lips when finished. He kissed her body wherever he was as he prepped Sofie and the instruments. This was the first time she had been fully exposed to him or any male in her life, and it was exciting, and embarrassing and oh, so deliciously naughty.

***

Taking his long leather ties, he attached her ankles to two end roll arm sofa legs, her thighs spread, knees on the sofa cushion, arse up, arms out but not tied so she could hold herself up. Her breasts dangling as plump, ripe pears ready for harvest that hung from the trees. Not uncomfortably restrained, but he had learned and remembered that if she were tied completely immobile, his Sofie panicked.

This was not a day bed where true comfort could be found for a long time. Sofie's breasts' position made the clothespins easier to attach to her poor nipples. The moment the bite of pain hit her system, her blood would heat and boil, her cunny would leak further, and her core would clench hard. Just what he wanted.

Suckling each nip and massaging her fleshing breasts, he attached first one pin, then the other each clamped nip would bring on a yelp of discomfort.

"Breathe, sweetheart."

Trenton encouraged her compliance with slow, easy breaths of his own as he slid his hands up and over her entire body. The pins were on the rosy, pink skin of her nipples. His sweetheart had asked to see an anatomy book once he'd started to play with her body. He hadn't allowed it.

"Anatomy books are not for young ladies."

Sofie had accepted his words, but he was sure that sometime when he was gone from the house, she had or would look at one. It was a tantalizing thought. Maybe they would peruse it together. His manhood stiffened even more.

"Ahh." Sofie inhaled and exhaled harshly.

This was a more sensitive placement than when he had simply put one mid-tit. Besides, this was Sofie's first time, and so she was more tender. He had included some of her dark skin surrounding her nipples. Maybe an anatomy book was a good idea. Sofie lifted up.

"Need to say your word?"

"Nooo," she whispered.

"Good girl."

***

The warmth from the pain settled in, and the chill from her exposure cooled her heated reactions. Sofie wanted to resist, but his hand, at the nape of her neck, firmly repositioned her, pressing her breasts down onto the sofa, her forearms the support now. A new rush of tingling pain erupted, and with no further warning, Sofie came hard, just on the strength of that play.

"Pain and pleasure. You need one to enhance the other." Trenton kissed and licked her cheek as she came down slowly. Then he tenderly touched his lips to hers, intimate, gentle. Loving? Sofia wanted more, but Trenton stepped back. His message was loud and clear. He was in control. And she wanted it and hated it.

"Naughty girl. This is punishment for being obstinate and moody. Now that your worst tension is relieved, my little lady is going to feel my punishment inside and out of her beautiful bottom."

She cried out as he played with her tits. Her arousal began to move upward as she endured his unclipping of her breasts, one at a time, leaning down to draw the nips in his mouth and sucking the blood flow back quickly. "We mustn't keep them on too long."

She bellowed out in surprise at the pain of releasing her from the pins. It was worse than before. The sheen of perspiration on her skin soon changed to a chill, and she shivered from the cold and what she knew was coming next.

Sofie watched as he took what looked like butter from a dish that had appeared out of nothing. It was smeared on her bottom hole, his fingers going deep and spreading wide, preparing her for the next bit of punishment. The stretching caused her core and her bottom to throb. Her dark entrance always brought her embarrassment when touched for cleansing, but when Trenton touched it, the riot of sensations was unmatched by anything else she had ever experienced. She immediately wanted him to do more and do less.

Next would be one of the many plugs he had. The heavy marble plug appeared enormous, but she had seen Trenton had many larger ones. This one was big with a long wide end before dipping to the flange where it would be seated in her bottom hole. Where she knew it would ultimately stay until he was done tormenting her so thoroughly, and she was exhausted from the orgasmic play.

The marble was cold, so cold. Sometimes, he had told her, he would warm it up, but that was Sofie play, not punishment. She wondered if she could endure the cold. This was Sofie play and punishment, so it was hard to guess what her Duke would do.

"It is cold because you are naughty, woman. I'm going to ream your little arse hole, stretching you, impaling you deep, wide, painfully. I want you to cry out your pain. I want you to acknowledge your lover is not happy with you, and you deserve this. Understood?"

His voice was stern, and yet, that tinge of tenderness was heard. There was no anger, no irritation. He was enjoying this as much as she was. Sofie experienced a love/hate relationship with this play, and while he was careful, she knew that if she used her word, he would stop. Her bottom stretched slowly, the pinch was sharp, and then there was the deeper twinge of pain. He had not forced her arse open this much the last time.

"Ah, too much, Trenton." She turned her head to see him.

He smiled at her use of his name. "No, not enough. Deep breath, sweetheart." His words eased her worry. "We are still playing, Sofie. Your punishment is only our play. Remember that love. I know you can endure it for the reward ahead."

He pushed a little more of the plug inside her darkest entrance, and she moaned the good ache and the slight pinch of pain. She grew more breathless. The sensations were overwhelming her already heavily taxed emotions. Holding the intruder in place, he slapped her bottom cheek hard, she screeched, and he did it again, over, and over while holding the instrument of torture and enjoyment in the same position.

The spanking stopped, and her chest slowed its labored movement. The sensations that were soon to overwhelm her receded enough to give her rest and yet frustrate her.

"Again," said Trenton.

The plug moved, and oh, the stretch. "Ah, sir, I am at my limit. You will surely tear me asunder."

"No, not even close, and you will be opened more before we seat this in your naughty darkness. Now, more. Scream if you must."

She would not scream. No, it was not proper. But the log-sized intruder in her backside was more than her body could accommodate, and with the next inch pressed further inside, she screamed, and he spanked her bottom hard and fast. She came with an almost violent jolt of reaction when he slapped her cunny, the wet splat heard over and over again, bringing with it an overwhelming embarrassment.

She came again when he shoved the plug further and flicked her painful, throbbing breasts, finishing with strikes to her upper thighs. Sofia thought she would stop, but the sensations seemed to go on forever. When she had relaxed as she came down enough to take in her surroundings again, Trenton kissed her lips hard and bit her neck sharply. Sofie whimpered.

"One last round before I seat this plug and dole out the remainder of your punishment."

"What? There is more?"

"A little. It is more comfortable now, right?"

She knew what he meant. He was right. The plug didn't feel overly large now after coming. "Right, last time. Scream, Sofia, scream."

And scream she did. She vocalized her orgasm long and loud while lifting up on her hands to pump her arse, impaling herself over and over on the giant plug. Trenton tweaked the closest overly sensitive nipple, then released to such a rush of feeling she couldn't think.

Her arse and thighs were painted with his handprints, and her cunny was slapped mercilessly. With every new sensation, she cried out, pounded into the plug and was totally out of her mind. He controlled her, dominated every part of her being. She was his to command.

"And now the strap."

She had nothing left, and the strap, while she could feel every line, every bit of contact, it was anticlimactical. He laid her flat on the settee to complete the strapping. It was almost comforting to lie, stretched out fully under his will, the cushions under her head, her breasts smashed against the firm upholstery, her backside accepting his easy thrashing. His delivery was almost tender.

As she lay there and felt each caressing length of the leather, Sofie realized that she'd genuinely needed this. She'd wanted it, craved it, and when she left him, she would never have it again. She could never trust another to protect her in this mad, addictive way as she trusted this man.

He landed the flat leather strap over her tender parts between her thighs, and the shock sent her nearly over the edge again. Sofie thought there was no way she could come another time. One more taste of the strap, not hard, but she was so tender there, it sent a rush of heat and pushed her into a rushing river of sensation.

She was drowning in the overpowering seizing of her muscles. Her lower entrances trembled. Even her mouth watered, and her lips tingled. The sensation was so intense that when Trenton caressed her thighs, she trembled in overwhelming awareness and a complete lack of control over her body. Trenton mastered her. She was ruined for any other man.

Finally, Sofie's body stopped trembling. Trenton's kisses were gentle. She would have said loving before today, but now she knew he was simply thanking her for allowing him his pleasures. Did he know they were now her pleasures as well? Probably, and maybe that was why she worked so well for him. Had worked so well. He drew a line in the sand and ended any possibility of her crossing to him.

Trenton slowly replaced his items, wrapped the butt plug in a cloth and redressed Sofie, having untied her at some point during the play. He returned to continue kissing and cooing, rubbing, and consoling her, telling her she was a good little lady, the best. It was what she needed to finish this game because she would never hear or play it again.

She was growing tired and knew he would carry her to bed as he had done before. How could he be so tender, so loving, and yet, have no love for her? As he gathered her in his arms, he kissed her forehead tenderly. The total security she felt in his arms was indescribable. A profound lethargy overcame her like it did right before sleep enveloped her. She had only this last opportunity to tell him her true feelings, so she took it as she dozed off to sleep.

"I love you, Trenton."

Chapter 13

When she awoke, Sofia felt the warmth of the sun as it shone in her bedroom window. She was in her nightdress, snuggled in her blankets, but she could only vaguely remember how she got there. Sofia lay in bed, thinking of what had transpired in Trenton's study. She wondered how she had actually wanted that behavior. She throbbed, pleasantly aching, everywhere. And entirely embarrassed!

How would she be able to show her face again? How could she eat at the table without reliving the deprivation, the total debauchery that their meal had turned into? And then, the library where the scene was completed created another reminder that sent her in a different mental direction.

As Sofia reviewed every wicked thing they had done and the wanton screams she had released at his behest, she smiled with slow appreciation of the remaining glow. Trenton had indeed beguiled her because even now, in the aftermath of their play, when she should have been devastated beyond measure at the utter loss of her innocence, all she could generate was a luscious sense of decadence.

Trenton had said he wouldn't take her virtue and promised he still hadn't, but what more could she lose? She was well and truly ruined for any other man. The actual act, he assured her, was even more satisfying, more decadent than any play they had engaged in. How could it be? She would surely expire from the hedonistic pleasures they had engaged in already. More? It could not be true.

Sofia should leave him immediately before she was too tangled in his web of debauched gratifications. She was bewildered at how she, a properly raised young lady, could have had the life experiences she'd had in such a short space of time. Even now, when she should be thinking of marriage to a proper husband, she preferred Trenton. He confused her and sent her heart pounding and her emotions reeling.

She suspected that he saw her as merely a plaything. A distraction he had called her. She was nothing more than a new toy to lavish all his attention on to then, when bored, begin to lose interest, lessening his time spent and finally, to cast aside for a new endeavor. And still, she was drawn to him, bound to him by some unseen force that engulfed her.

She was the shiny bauble he was focused on now, but as he had become more used to her, he had turned to his perceived obligation. Trenton was already looking to end what they had barely begun. And the arrogance of powerful men. He might soon become bored with her as a plaything, but to make her his ward! How impertinent! She was now bound to him even tighter with no relief in sight.

She would not be a burden, and while she had agreed to his help, she'd made the devastating error of growing to love Trenton more, not less. Her desires had morphed into having a long-term arrangement rather than a temporary one. That was her problem. Her mistake. Trenton was doing as he promised. She had changed, not he. No time like the present to right that error in judgment.

Arriving at the breakfast table, fully dressed and her hair put up in a simple twist, Sofia sat and ate a small, tasteless meal while deciding which of her new friends she should beg assistance. Not Cairis, the woman was pregnant whether she was ready to admit the reality or not. That left a pang in her heart for what she had thought was part of her future with the Duke. No, Sofia was not risking any harm come to her.

Annalise was too confident that all things could be worked out if one simply tried. Not the right philosophy for this. Then there was Rosemary. She appeared to be the most benevolent. She might be willing to step out on a limb because, after all, she had been raised in The Colonies-

America and her husband was the least intense of the men she had recently met. No, she wouldn't ask Rosemary. She might want to go with Sofia to help protect her.

Genevieve would be her target. Lord Kendrick might rule his home with an iron fist, but he loved his wife to distraction. It was there for all to see. He also seemed to give Genevieve enough freedom not to immediately notice if she had a hidden guest or if she took a little longer at the shops.

Now, to inquire of Trenton when he intended to leave for his affairs elsewhere. Trenton, as it turned out, was not at home. She found Mr. Kerns, who thought she was distressed at not finding His Grace, sought to reassure Lady Montclair.

"Now that you are His Grace's ward, he requires you to stay home until your tutor arrives tomorrow. He advises he will be gone some days while he completes business."

Disappointed at not seeing him before he left but relieved that she would have some time to work out the details, Sofia sat at the small secretariat desk to gather her thoughts. Taking a cleansing breath, she sent a note to Lady Kendrick and requested that she see her as soon as possible. That good lady sent her a reply quickly, encouraging her to come at her convenience. She would be home all day. Sofia found Trudy and made plans for the visit.

The two young women arrived at Lord Kendrick's home within the hour, and once they were seated, Sofia plunged into her dilemma.

"Genevieve, I must tell you something in the strictest of confidences."

That good lady acted as though there were no issues whatsoever with keeping a secret from her husband and her other friends. Sofia hoped that was true as she explained her error in falling for His Grace and the actions he had taken on her behalf, namely the guardianship.

"Oh, my dear, you are in quite a pickle. But be assured, we have all commented on how enamored His Grace is of you. Indeed, he must have told our husbands the same, for they say his original plans have changed."

Sofia shook her head sadly. "I fear they are incorrect except that I am now his ward." As Sofia explained what she could, trying to be as transparent in her meaning as possible, Genevieve commiserated with her.

"Yes, we are most vulnerable when we have first given our hearts. There is no assurance the feelings are reciprocated. And in your case, the Duke has surely appeared to not return your affections in his choice of deeds if not in his overall manner towards you. He treats you as his own. He chastises as if it matters, and if he thought of you as less than his, then he would not have introduced us. It is confusing, indeed."

"I had thought the same, but as his ward, I would think that to be appropriate," reasoned Sofia.

"No, I disagree. His Grace's behavior does not at all seem appropriate for a guardian/ward relationship. He has paid an inordinate amount of attention to every personal and private detail concerning you. I guarantee that is something he would not have done with his ward. He has chastised you as though it were important. A mere ward would not have been treated so personally by His Grace after such a short time. Oh, he would have seen to your comfort and your protection but not personally. And if he has called you his little one or by a little name, then I believe he has other reasons to have gained guardianship over you, not for the reason you fear."

Sofia didn't want to contradict the very woman she was here to ask for assistance, so she appeared to listen. Sofia was positive she had come to the right conclusion. The Duke wasn't yet tired of her, but he anticipated to need to shift her soon. Whether that be to a genteel position or a husband, it mattered not to him. They had more conversation before Genevieve shook her head at what Sofia said the tutor was hired to do.

"Teach you how to what? Catch a husband? Oh, my, he is off the path there. You don't need help in that realm, and in fact, you have your husband if he would but see it."

"Yes, so now you see, I must save face and preserve my reputation. I will need to find a place to go. I had thought to go to America, but Rosemary has shared enough of life there that I'm afraid I would not prosper."

"No, I quite agree. How about going to the duke's country estate?"

"I have never been there, of course, nor do I think many are in residence at this time."

"No, but that would give you more time to figure things out. His Grace is gone for some days, and you would go where you would be welcomed. I am sure there is some kind of paper to prove who you say you are. His ward would be most welcome. Take your maid. She will also vouch for you, and they would believe her, being a staffer they already know."

The ladies finished their tea and decided to give it another day. "Or, I could say I'm going there and go somewhere else."

"That's all fine and well in conversation, but a woman never does well when traveling alone to unknown destinations. Cairis attempted to go to her own home alone, and it proved dangerous. If her Cullen had not found her quickly…" Genevieve shivered. "And I have gone in the darkest of nights, only to be nearly killed accidentally by Kendrick. No, I will secure your travel to Trenton Hall."

"But what if he returns?" Sofia's gloves were fisted in her hands and hopelessly crumpled.

"He always stays the season. And if you are right, he is still in search of a wife. He will stay until the season's end. If you are wrong, I hope you can sit by the season's end. He did commission that beautiful gown for the last ball."

Sofia ignored any perceived evidence of his deeper affection than she had already attributed to him. "Good. Then I shall go tomorrow before that dreaded tutor arrives. Tomorrow, bright and early. Send me the information I shall need this evening."

"You will need money."

"He has given me pin money I have not used. I know where Trenton keeps more besides. I'll leave a note so that he does not accuse anyone of thievery. Never fear on that score. I have lived on no coin at all before, so I shall be fine. I imagine I will need a small amount, however, to take care of Trudy. How much should I take with me?"

The women itemized costs and then doubled them to include the maid's meals and estimated the arrival time. Satisfied, Sofia gathered her maid and returned home. She would need to pack.

Later that evening, as Sofia finished her supper in a room that was suspiciously unattended by a maid or footman, she heard Mr. Kerns speaking to a man at the door. It sounded like her brother, his voice booming loudly, which was often the case after too much drink. Sofia raced up the side staircase to catch a glimpse.

"She is my sister, and I demand to see her."

"I am sorry, Lord Cloverfield, but I'm sure I do not know of whom you speak. The Duke of Trenton lives here with his ward. That is all."

"No, I was told Sofia was here by a man who would not lead me down a Banbury path. Her own cousin, no less. Let me see her. I have her betrothed waiting on her."

Sofia was devastated at hearing such a lie, but would Mr. Kerns believe her or the Baron of Cloverfield? She had no idea, but Mrs. Kerns would not be easily convinced by either. She would have to beseech the woman to hear her out and then try to get away. That dear woman knew too much of what went on in the Duke's household to do less.

"You will have to leave. If you wish to speak to The Duke of Trenton, he should be back in a week. Please leave your card, and I will make sure he gets your message."

"Let me speak to his ward, then."

"That is not possible. His ward is under the Duke's protection. Only those approved by His Grace may be entertained."

"I will get my sister out of your clutches. The duke has no hold stronger than a brother's."

Mr. Kerns stood firmly at the door and did not allow Robert in, but Sofia knew that nothing would forestall him for long if her brother was adamant. She would have to leave in the morning, but maybe she would be able to garner assistance now since Robert had made such a loud nuisance of himself.

She would have to tell a bit of a yarn, but certainly, she would be forgiven. Trenton surely would not hold it against her. Her buttock clenched at the thought of his retribution should he find her too soon. She hoped he didn't.

Now she would need to get away for sure. If Robert had found her a suitor, it could not have been for a good reason nor for her benefit. He had something planned, and she could be certain it was in his favor and not hers. There was nothing to do but send a message to Genevieve and see if she could secure two carriage seats quickly.

Sofia sent the footman with the message to be delivered to Lady Genevieve. She spent precious time sitting with Mrs. Kerns and explained her real story about what happened to her, paying special attention to Robert's involvement.

"Let me get things straight in my mind. This man who came to find you is, indeed, your brother. He left you to your own devices for survival while he sold your family home, took all the assets and fled the country over some gambling debts he was unable or unwilling to pay?"

"Yes. And Robert sold our home to our cousin, who would be next in line for the title if my brother died. He agreed to pay for the house if we were both gone from it. This is why I was living the way I was when His Grace found me."

Mr. Kerns announced that Ladies Thayer, Ashton, O'Leary, and Kendrick were in the receiving room waiting for Her Ladyship. He ended the announcement with a frown of decided disapproval for the lateness of the hour and the women being unaccompanied except by themselves.

Mrs. Kerns urged her toward the door. "Go on, Lass, and speak with your friends. Mr. Kerns will work on getting word to His Grace. You will promise me that you will not leave. We can only protect you if you are here. And our Duke won't know where to find you if you are in the world without protection."

"Yes, milady. Agree to the promise. His Grace is entirely unmanageable if he has been openly defied on something he was adamant about. In this case, that is for you to remain home and safe."

"But what about my brother and whomever he has gotten to marry me? He is my brother and has that right."

"Ah, but now that His Grace has guardianship over you, it is expected that your brother would have to answer to the magistrate as to why he left you to find a way to survive after he took all the family funds. I imagine his choice of a husband will be disregarded. Especially when His Grace explains you are meant to marry him."

"I don't know that is true, Mrs. Kerns. There is so much that points in another direction."

"Aye, you trust my word. I've known our Duke for a long time, and it is true."

"And what about the tutor His Grace has hired." There just seemed no end to the dilemmas these days.

"You let me take care of that, my girl. You go have a nice chat and see what the young ladies have to say. But first, I will have your promise."

Sofia frowned. Could she make that promise if she were planning on leaving? No. But Mrs. Kerns made some excellent points. She had known Trenton for a very long time. If she took care of the tutor so that Sofia did not have to be subjected to the instruction of how to procure a husband, Sofia would be forever in Mrs. Kerns' debt.

"Yes, alright, I promise. For now."

"That's a good child. I'll send in the tea soon." The older woman gave Sofie a small smile and patted her hand before shooing her off.

Sofia impulsively hugged her benefactor. "Thank you for helping me, Mrs. Kerns."

Sofia took a deep breath and crossed the threshold to the little receiving room she used for a sitting room, and the conversation stopped immediately. After about five seconds of a lull, the room burst again with chatter aimed at Sofie.

"We don't have time to dilly-dally. My Lord Kendrick will be home in a few hours."

"Yes, we all need to be quick. I would say we can stay one hour only, then we must be on our way home. Lord Ashton is a man of habit, but even he can break from his traditional behaviors on occasion," said Rosemary.

Annalise spoke to the crux of the reason they were there at such an hour. "We must insist that you stay home. Your brother, if we are to understand, is a danger to you. I'm not sure how, exactly, but we all feel he wishes nothing in the way of your happiness."

At just that moment, a light tea was served. Sofia began to pour when the maid who had brought the tea returned to announce that a gentleman by the name of Lord Cragas was in the foyer, waiting to speak to milady.

"I don't know who that is, Jane. Do not say I am at home. Inquire as to his business and possibly have him return when His Grace is in residence."

"Yes, milady."

When Jane returned, she announced that the gentleman said, "he would see you soon."

"How odd," said Sofia.

"Don't see him, whoever he is. He is likely attached to your brother. Trenton would be extremely irritated if you spoke to someone you don't know without him present. I don't have to live in this house to know that would not be a good idea."

"Maybe I should just go," said Sofia.

"And go where?" asked Cairis. "There is nowhere safe for an unaccompanied woman and certainly not much better with her maid. I speak with great authority on that. The Laird has yet to get over my attempts at saving him and myself by a similar method. It has been nearly two years. Trust me when I say that when your Duke finds you, as they always do, you will be in Dutch for a long time."

"Yes, Cairis is right. We will protect you. You can come to our homes one at a time until the Duke is found," offered Genevieve. "We can offer that shelter. If you go off alone or even with a maid, we cannot be of any assistance when things go awry as they always do."

"Oh, but you will be in so much trouble if you are found to be hiding me."

"No, protecting you. There is a great deal of difference," said Rosemary. "One is expected to assist one's friends, are they not? Ashton cannot be at odds with me there, for he has stepped into the fray many times for his own friends."

"Absolutely," declared Annalise. "Thayer has as well. We are just taking a page from our husbands' books. Now, who shall go first? I certainly could if you like. Yes, you are to stay with us for several days, maybe a week, because we do not know when Trenton will return. You say you're lonely. Our papas would never allow a little lady to be frightened. And now that we have had your brother and then a stranger ask for you, the men will demand you stay under their roof. Yes, it will do nicely."

"Perfect," agreed Cairis. "And we have obligations that you have yet to have, so you are better suited to simply come and stay with us than we are to take time out of our daily schedule and come visit."

"Oh, Ashton would believe that. He would agree that Sofia should come to us rather than his wife go to Sofia's every day to check up on her. Better to keep a watchful eye as is his want."

"Kendrick would be delighted if I spent some time with another friend he approves of. I seem to have a few unsavory friends, as Kendrick calls them, and he is forever trying to steer me to a higher class of people. A future duchess of his partner and friend fits the bill nicely."

"Right. We should go, but I shall expect you to come over tomorrow to stay a week," announced Annalise.

"Yes, I will, but not a week, surely. A few days should suffice. His Grace shouldn't be gone so long that I would need to spend a week with each one of you, would he? And Robert will give up. Right?"

"Quite likely. I'll make sure my Lord Thayer gets a message to the Duke," said Annalise.

"And this plan will save you from a sore behind," said Rosemary. "The best of outcomes, really."

"Likely saving you from many," added Genevieve. "That previous plan would have left you perpetually standing."

"And it is always prudent to avoid an angry sir," added Cairis.

"Yes, Sofia, it is so much better than having to explain why you thought taking a coach, unprotected, to his family home or anywhere was a good idea," added Cairis.

"Alright, you've convinced me. I'll do it."

Chapter 14

Trenton hated to leave Sofia when she was so vulnerable, but he had to take care of her family issues before marrying her. The biggest problem at the moment was her brother. Next was to find out about her parents. He had procured a few well-respected tracker services in the hopes of finding either the parents or information on their graves and the brother's whereabouts. His solicitor was also tapping his resources in the government.

He had thought to spend time destroying the brother's credentials because that is what Devil Dukes were expected to do, and it would grant him a modicum of satisfaction. Unfortunately, Trenton could see the man had already done worse himself, so no satisfaction there.

Next, he had intended to go to Sofia's family home but ultimately decided against it. The cousin in residence was already wary of him after their first meeting. It would do no one any good to allow him the satisfaction of proclaiming that the Devil Duke was indeed the devil incarnate. He had other ways to make things unpleasant for the man who refused to keep Sofia in residence even though that same event brought her into the Duke's life.

Sofia had a home with him now, and while it was sad for her, and he would have wanted to give her back the home she grew up in, it would have been fruitless. Although decorated with brocade-covered walls and carpeted floors, what good would empty rooms be if Sofia's family, her parents, were not in residence? The possession would be as hollow as the house. No, his time would be better used gaining his marriage license, waiting on the reply from the scouts and dealing with the brother and the final settling of Sofia's parent's state of affairs.

He spent time with the solicitor, setting up an account and changing paperwork that stated, once they were married, all the ordinary and usual things would belong to Sofia if Trenton died before her. Should they be blessed with any, their children would have a secure future befitting a duke's offspring. He spent time with the church representative and had the banns readings set for the following three Sunday services.

Staying at his club overnight helped him to stay focused on the business at hand. While his affairs in London were working through, he went to Trenton Hall in Trenton on Lea, Sussex, to speak to his mother. The woman had stopped giving advice, but she did touch on Trenton's need to marry and begat an heir or three. His mother felt that was an obligation she could not shirk.

"Exeter, darling, what brings you back from London so soon?" asked the Dowager Trenton.

His mother, who named him Exeter and was the only one allowed to use that name, didn't seem overly concerned that he had returned, just curious. That was how she was since Trenton had prematurely taken his father's place in the family.

"I have something to discuss with you before I make a commitment."

The Dowager clapped her hands. "You have found a woman who you want to marry."

"How do you do that? You have no word or indication that there is something afoot, and yet you know immediately." Trenton shook his head and kissed his mother on the cheek before standing and walking around the drawing room. "I want you to come back with me, so you are at the wedding. If you are up to the trip, that is. Sofia would love to meet you. You are very similar in temperament and mannerisms."

"Sofia, what a lovely name. And I would love to go, but I do so hate London, and you plan to bring my new daughter straight here, I presume?"

"Within a few weeks, most certainly by the end of the Spring Season. I have to end my business before returning for the winter. If Sofia is pregnant soon, then we won't be going back for at least a year. Maybe longer. I will be obligated to make a couple of short trips, of course."

"I need something stronger than tea, Exeter. I'll take some whiskey and water, please."

Trenton stared at his mother for a moment before a slow smile crossed his face. "If you are sure, Mother."

"I am. This is exciting news. Now get me my drink and sit beside me. Tell me about your lovely Sofia."

Trenton poured his mother's drink, careful to put twice the amount of water to whiskey as his mother rarely imbibed.

"Now, tell me what she looks like and what drew you to her. I want to know everything."

Trenton told of Sofia's rich brown curls and the dreadful time she had trying to keep them under control. Then he described her innocent nature protected by her witty tongue. An innocence he had defiled and soon would have taken her to completion if he had stayed there. That last bit of information, he kept wisely to himself.

"She can be a handful at times, but she keeps me on my toes. There is never a dull moment." He smiled again.

"She makes you happy. I know because you have smiled more in this short visit than you have in any week before meeting her. She is good for you." She patted his hand. "I don't need to meet her to know that. You marry your Sofia and let her make you happy. I have wanted that for you, my dear. Bring her home with you as soon as you are able."

"Thank you, Mother, I will."

"Good. Sofia must have your grandmother's ring."

"Are you sure? I mean to have one of them for her, but it doesn't have to be grandmother's wedding ring."

"Of course it does. We will retrieve it before you leave. Now, talk to me about what I need to have done in this house in preparation for you to bring your bride home."

The rest of the next few days were full of instructions and catching up on things that came up while he was gone. His staff was very good at what they did and were used to taking over when he was away, but Trenton wanted to be sure there were no huge issues to greet them as soon as they arrived. He wanted to take the time to show Sofia around the estate and teach her about their home when they finally arrived.

Trenton worked non-stop to prepare things, and when he was finished, he slept for ten hours before taking his leave from his mother. As his coach pulled away from the Hall, Trenton noticed a lone rider on the side of the lane. No one came down that lane unless they were going to the Hall. The road ended at the gates.

Trenton had his driver halt as they were in the gate entrance. "Ho there. Who do you seek?" he asked of the rider.

"Trenton Hall. I was told that Lord Trenton resided here."

"The Duke of Trent resides here. I am his brother. Can I help you?" Trenton was never one to shy away from the truth or handling an issue, but he had a strange feeling about this man. It would be better to tread carefully for now.

"Excellent! Is your brother at home?"

"Alas, you have missed him. He left for the continent more than a month ago. He and his new bride should be arriving in London within the week."

"His bride? Who is that?" The man's countenance changed to a fearful concern.

"I don't think we have exchanged introductions, so if you would be so kind, Sir, I would have your name."

"Yes, yes." Suddenly the man seemed less than enthusiastic and more annoyed. "Lord Robert Cloverfield."

"Cloverfield? Out of London? My new sister-in-law is from London as well. Lady Sofia Cloverfield. Duchess Trenton now, of course. Are you related?"

The look of total disbelief, then anger, followed by dejection, and finally fear. Trenton could imagine all of those things to be true. As much as he wanted to tear Sofia's brother limb from limb, it wasn't to be. He would have to allow him to live a while longer.

"What did you want Trenton for? I might be able to aid you in your endeavors."

The man shot Trenton a disgruntled stare. "Not unless you can undo the marriage my sister and your brother have embarked upon."

"Happily, no. But Trenton and your sister will be returning within the week, and I am sure you will be welcome in their home. I would give them a week, a fortnight for sure, and then you will be likely to see them. I'm sure your sister must have wondered what happened to you after you left her in London."

Trenton was so close to revealing too much. Better he left but not until he took the man with him. He could put up with his company a little longer if it meant he took him away from the estate and possibly bother the Dowager.

"I don't suppose there is anyone at home?"

"Oh, plenty but none of the family. Once these gates are closed, no one will be received until Trenton returns next month. We have armed groundskeepers and a great Scottish Gillie to protect the property. Now, I can show you to an outstanding boarding house about—"

A gun went off, likely bird shooting but no need to clarify. The sound lent credence to his earlier words. Trenton was happy that the message was received by Cloverfield.

"Yes, I can see what you mean. I'll be off."

"Well, just stay on this road going back towards London, and you will see the establishment in about an hour. The Dog and Hare."

"Yes, thank you. I stayed the night there last evening. I think I will take a short rest and then continue on back to London."

Cloverfield trotted back in the direction from which he came. It was difficult to let him go unharmed, but it was for the best. Hopefully, Sofia's brother would take off for the continent again and not bother her anymore. Trenton returned to the hall long enough to tell his Gillie what had transpired. That good man would go about the place and make sure everyone knew about the encounter and to watch for Robert, should he return.

Finally finished with his notifications, Trenton began his trip back to London, and with any luck, back to news he had been waiting on. Sofia would be glad to see him when he told her of what he had learned. If the heavens were in agreement, she would not have driven the tutor completely mad before he could come and release the poor woman. Just the thought of how his Fia was dealing with the tutor was enough to get him the last few miles to his stopover.

Trenton was tired. They had put in two good, long days, but he and his driver needed sleep. The horses needed rest as well. Stopping at the tavern he usually stayed in, Trenton ordered supper and a bed for both himself and his driver. The coachman took his dinner with Trenton and his bed where the other coachmen slept.

Trenton was sitting in the corner, enjoying watching a game of cards, when he overheard an older gentleman speaking of how stupid he was to allow his daughter to stay behind in England instead of going with his wife and him to India.

"My daughter was of age, but still, she had no protection other than her brother, and I have learned that he was less than protective."

Trenton moved closer and soon was sitting on one side of the gentleman. He felt compelled to introduce himself because this was, very likely, Sofia's father.

"Hello. I hope I'm not intruding on your conversation, but I am the Duke of Trenton, and I believe we have someone in common."

Trenton couldn't believe his luck. Evidently, Robert Cloverfield had sent his parents a message that Sofia had gone on holiday with her friend to the Continent. She would be gone a year. After another six months, the Indian assignment was over, and Lord and Lady Cloverfield returned to England.

His Lordship returned to find his home, no longer his home. The staff was turned out, and his nephew was installed in Cloverfield House.

"Evidently, Robert gambled away his money and all of Sofia's that was left for her while we were gone. He even sold the house to my nephew. When I walked into my home and saw it was taken over by that wastrel, I sent my dear wife off in a carriage to her friend while I sorted things out."

"I can imagine the shock you must have endured."

"I fear you would be sorely lacking in understanding of the strength of emotions I had to subdue, to conduct business. After finding out what my son did, I asked my nephew how he could have paid for our home without verifying I was deceased. The mongrel said that he had wanted the family home. 'It is one of the largest in London,' he said.

"I told him to get out. I was firm but polite, of course. I told him that I was sorry for his unfortunate business with my son, but he would have to remove his possessions by evening tomorrow. And take only his things. He asked about the money that he had spent on purchasing the property. I sent the opportunistic heathen to find Robert and get it back from him. Blood from a turnip if you know my meaning."

Trenton explained the unpleasant encounter he had with Robert two days before. "I hope Sofia had the good sense not to speak to him outside of my presence."

"Why would he even think she would see him after what he did to her?"

"Sofia has a tender heart and is a forgiving sort, as I am sure you remember. She wouldn't want to break off all ties to her brother if she thought he was the only family she had left. I believe once she sees her parents are alive, that Robert won't have the same hold on her as he did previously."

"My daughter does not hold grudges, but things may have changed since her horrific experiences. I can scarce imagine the terror she must have felt." Lord Cloverfield said.

"Yes, I am sure the ordeal changed her, but as I've only known her since that time. I have nothing to base my thoughts on except now. However, I know that if your son was looking for me in Sussex, he must have wanted her pretty badly. I fear it was to use her again for his own gain. Her virtue is still intact, you see. I have made sure of that once I discovered as much. How she was able to accomplish that, I have no idea, but she did."

Trenton filled in the details of the life Sofia had led since being turned out by her brother. Her father was appropriately horrified. Trenton felt a modicum of satisfaction that the Baron appeared to realize the unforgivable way Sofia was abandoned. For what man left his unattached daughter to go abroad for an extended period, unattended? There must have been some thought as to the morality of his son. Trenton ended the tale on a different note.

"Sofia is happy and healthy and soon to be my wife."

"Well, young man, I have yet to give permission."

"True, but I have also procured guardianship over her to protect her against those who would do her harm. We will be married in just over two weeks. You would not be able to get your case and complaint to be answered in that time. Your daughter has endured so much, Lord Cloverfield. It would be better for Sofia if you were simply happy for her."

"I hear your words, but I must speak to her before I agree."

"Understood. I love your daughter, and it is my belief that she loves me. You shall see for yourself. I'm eager to return home to her, as I am sure you are eager to reunite. Shall we meet in the morning and continue on to my home near Grosvenor's Square?"

"Excellent."

By early afternoon, the two men arrived in Trenton's coach, intent on seeing Sofia and assuring themselves of her safety. Trenton led the way inside and was met by a distraught Mrs. Kerns, a militant Mr. Kerns, a weepy Trudy, and a complaining tutor but no Sofia.

Trenton gathered all the key participants into his library. He poured whiskey for him, Mr. Kerns and Lord Cloverfield. They were just getting Trudy to turn off the waterworks and the tutor to stop demanding to meet Sofia when four more men joined the chaos. Thayer looked at the room full of people and turned to Trenton.

"Thank God you are here. Have you found your Sofia yet?"

"What? Found her? Is she lost? What the bloody hell is going on here?" demanded the Devil Duke.

"Your Grace, I may be able to start the story," said Mrs. Kerns.

Trenton waved toward the drink and nodded to his friends to help themselves, which they did without hesitation. Trudy began to wail again. "Trudy, you will stop that caterwauling this instant, do you hear me?"

"Yes, Your Grace." The girl did try but was not completely successful.

"I have been here for more than a week, waiting on your return so that I may meet my pupil. I am not in the habit of being made to wait. I am a respectable tutor, having worked for the finest—"

"Enough!" thundered Trenton. "You obviously have nothing to add to the current conversation as you have never met my Sofia, so retire to your room, please, and I shall send for you directly."

He was not often ignored, and the tutor must have understood that, for she stood with quite a bit of muted attitude and walked, with an air of wounded pride, from the room.

Trenton turned to his housekeeper. "Now, Mrs. Kerns, what have you to say."

That good lady recounted all Sofia had told her and the ensuing and subsequent conversations between the ladies and Sofia. She explained they were trying to keep her ladyship safe by keeping her from the house.

"I thought you said she was safe in your home," said Lord Cloverfield.

"She was… she is. It is obviously her brother whom she is not safe from. Allow the full events to be explained, please." Trenton turned back to Mrs. Kerns. "When was the last time you spoke to Lady Montclair."

"Cloverfield," corrected her father.

"Yes." Trenton loved Sofia, but her father was beginning to wear on his nerves. "When Mrs. Kerns?"

"Last evening. Her ladyship had come back to leave her soiled clothing and to gather new. Milady said she hoped you would return home soon, and she didn't have to stay away much longer. She was weary of sleeping in unfamiliar bedrooms and not spending evenings with Your Grace. No matter how good the company and how well-appointed the accommodations were, they were not as good as home. That is the last I saw of the wee lass." Mrs. Kerns, stoic and commanding to her staff, had obviously grown fond of Sofia, for her voice trembled on the last sentence.

"But she must have had a carriage waiting on her, right Kerns?" Trenton had turned to the butler.

"Yes, Your Grace. Lord Thayer's carriage was waiting for Lady Cloverfield."

Trenton turned to his friend. "Thayer, where the devil is she?"

Chapter 15

"I checked the coaches. She never came back out of the house." Trenton turned back to Kerns.

"That is correct, Your Grace. The footman came in to inquire after milady, and I sent Trudy up to find out if her ladyship was well." Trudy began blubbering again.

"Trudy, I shall find a strap if you start that crying up again. It isn't helping find Sofia."

"No, Your Grace. Beg pardon." She sniffed hard a few times, inhaled, and exhaled twice before speaking. "When I went up, Lady Sofia's clothes were tossed all over the room, which isn't like her. She is so careful of all the fine things you have bought her. She wrote with her rouge the words: *C-R-A-G-S and C-L-R-K-N-W-L*, on her dressing table."

Trenton, followed by the rest of the library's inhabitants, went to Sofia's room and saw what was written on the furniture. Crag with maybe an 's' after it and Clrknwl. He sat on her bed and thought. Clerkenwell, the workhouse she had been in for a few days before slipping out. What "Crag-s" meant Trenton could only guess it was someone's name. What was the name of the man who had attacked his Sofie?

He stood quickly. "Mr. and Mrs. Kerns, find out if any staff saw a man or woman or Sofia today. Most especially, anyone that would coincide with her disappearance." Those two left the room.

"Trudy, leave the rouge but clean the rest of your mistress' room and take anything that might be of interest or odd to Mrs. Kerns."

"Your Grace?" Trudy picked up a tiny bit of ripped stationery of Sofia's. It had "Trenton" with a heart she had colored in with her rouge. She was likely doing that when she was interrupted by this Crag-s person.

Trenton left the room behind the Kerns, who were briskly going about his orders. Now there were his friends and Sofia's father.

"We will go to Clerkenwell, and you, Sir, should stay here in case she returns before us. We will split up as needed, but I need someone Sofie is familiar with to stay here."

"Now see here—"

"You are familiar to her. Will you do that for your daughter?" Trenton was not a man to be defied at this moment. Cloverfield must have seen that, for he agreed.

"Well, when you put it that way, how can I refuse. Hurry back soon with her, Trenton."

"I intend to do my best," replied a worried Trenton.

The men raced to Clerkenwell and found they must line a few pockets with coins before acquiring the information they need. "But you won't find him," said the informant.

Ashton stared hard at the man. "Why is that?"

The grubby man shrugged. "Because he took his lady to America. Their ship left today."

Trenton looked hard at the man and then at O'Leary. "What is the schedule for the Dame America?"

"Aye, that is leaving today but not for another hour. We can make it. Maybe."

The twenty-minute carriage ride took thirty and felt like hours. The whole time, two stoic men sat beside Trenton while Thayer's carriage carried the other two. Looking out the window at the darkening sky, Trenton couldn't stop thinking of the horrors his little one had endured already.

How could Sofia be so gentle with such terrible experiences? And sassy. He fucking loved her sass. He didn't deserve someone so perfect for him. He would corrupt her, had corrupted her, but he was going to take her anyway. He would show his little darling duchess that he was worthy of her love. He would make her happy and give her babies, security, and love. Yes, he loved her. While it wasn't fashionable in his circles, he did love her, and she loved him if the little heart drawing meant anything.

"There it is. Thank God it's still docked," said Kendrick.

"Right. Kendrick, try to get some signal sent to the ship while we climb on board. And let the others know." Kendrick nodded and exited the carriage.

The Devil Duke and the Black Laird exited the carriage and ran toward the ship. They were an impressive duo pounding down the dock pier. The gangplank had been pulled, and it took O'Leary's bellowing voice to get one of the crew's attention. Five minutes later, with Ashton and Thayer behind them, they climbed the gangplank and spoke to the crew.

The crew, who knew they had only a short time left to find this man and woman and get them off the ship before they had to leave, split up and accompanied each lord. The sailors were intimately knowledgeable about their ship, and while O'Leary, Thayer, and Ashton were familiar, Kendrick and Trenton were not.

With the sailors watching all the exiting stairwells, the searchers went through every room systematically. As they approached a cabin at the end of a row of tiny staterooms, noises could be heard and then a woman's muffled scream. The crew knocked and asked if everything was alright.

"I need to see your passage ticket again. There appears to be only one passenger on it."

"I paid for two," came the hard, gruff reply.

"Nonetheless, sir, I need to see your ticket to verify.

The door was wrenched open, and a dirty belligerent man was standing in the entryway, posturing as though he were the king, himself. The next moment, that same man was falling forward as though he'd been shoved into the gangway. Trenton, who stood directly in the doorway, took the brunt of the man's descent.

Trenton recognized this man as the one who attacked his Sofia when he took her home. Things began to fall into place quickly, but he had no time to dwell on those revelations as the man lost his balance and fell into them heavily. Trenton caught a glimpse of his darling as she scaled the kidnapper's body and fell onto Trenton's chest. Instead of holding tightly, Sofia kept climbing over him as though she didn't notice who she had landed on. She scrambled through the crowd, racing down the passageway, tripping, and clawing her way toward the ladders.

***

Sofia heard an unfamiliar man call another's name, Cragas, and the voice that chilled her to the bone growled in angry response outside her rooms. Sofia knew immediately that she was in trouble. She'd no time to do more than quickly write some letters on the furniture, hoping that the letters made sense. That Trenton had listened to her story well enough to decipher their meaning in time. The men entered her room. With little means of fighting two men successfully, it didn't take much to drag her from the suite and toward the back of the house.

Once Sofia had been taken through the servant's quarters at knifepoint, she realized she only had two choices. Being stabbed in the side bringing on a most certain death or play-along until she found a vantage point to gain her freedom. There were no servants on the staircase, save the man dressed in Trenton's staff livery, indicating an opportunist accomplice amongst the Duke's employees. These corridors and steps were always busy this time of the day.

"Looking for saving, my dear? Unfortunately for you, there is a distraction in the front of the house, so we will exit without being stopped."

Sofia chose not to answer. Yes, it was all about timing. If she hadn't come to change her clothes and get the news of Trenton, she would not have been here at the precise time necessary to make her vulnerable. If this weren't the day for the staff meeting held in the kitchen, she wouldn't have been kidnapped.

If Trenton weren't gone, he would have been able to protect her. Now, if the ship didn't leave for America on just this day and if the crew were not already behind, Sofia might have been able to get away. Too many perfectly wrong events may be more that needed to take her far from her Duke and far from the home she had begun to feel it was hers.

Sofia feared all was lost regardless of her escape, for time was not on her side. Things looked grim. She had never learned to swim, so jumping would have decided her fate as quickly as staying on board. Trenton may not have been located in time. No one else knew of the place she had been, not even the friends she had cultivated. Mrs. Kerns would not be able to link the two incidents together. Her hope lay in Trenton.

Sofia hadn't told Mrs. Kerns the man's name in the workhouse because, until today, she did not know it. She wished she had tried to pay more attention, then she would have been alerted when the lunatic showed up at the house. Now Sofia knew it for sure. She had heard his name from his accomplice. Cragas was even wilder and crazier than he was at the workhouse, and she was confident he was the one who had attacked her when she lived in the dock area. Her fear was consuming.

And then the opportunity presented itself. The ship had not yet sailed. And wasn't Trenton one of the men who owned this ship? He and his friends? Yes, there was hope, but she was not waiting on the manifestation of that hope any longer. Sofia knew she would have to act now before the ship sailed.

It was apparent that Cragas did not have his sea legs yet. Sofia didn't either, but she could handle the anchored boat's gentle rocking better than Cragas. He had already set the knife down to steady himself and fight the first waves of nausea that overcame him. Now to find a way out of the door.

Then, with a better stroke of timing, the door was knocked on hard. Once Cragas opened it, Sofia was ready. She took the knife and slit the leather that was holding up his grungy trousers. Down they slipped. She dropped the knife and pushed hard. As he toppled forward, she climbed over the bumbling man, ignoring the stench, and scrambled with all her effort to get over whatever was in her path. She headed to the open deck and freedom.

Shouts and yelling erupted all around her as she clawed her way up the ladder to the chilly, salty breeze overhead. Bursting onto the deck, Sofia gathered her torn skirts higher and searched frantically for the gangplank.

"Sofia, Sofia, here!" yelled a familiar voice. Lord Thayer. And then a soothing voice with a distinctly Scottish lilt spoke gently to her immediate right.

"There, there, lass. We have your Duke coming for you. Let me have your hand, my dear."

"Laird?"

"Aye, lass." She flew to him, not caring for propriety when safety and protection could be found in his arms.

"Shh, little one. Your Papa is close at hand."

"Where is Trenton?" She held firmly to her last bit of restraint. The tears were barely held at bay.

"Coming towards you now. Turn around, lass. He is here."

"Sofia." Trenton's voice was desperate.

She turned, leaving the Laird and ran to Trenton's open arms. The reunion was tearful, and Trenton's kiss stole her breath. Someone cleared their throat, prompting the two to disengage when they wanted anything but release from the other.

"My Lords, we need to set the sail. Can we ask you to disembark the ship now?" asked an impatient First Mate.

"Yes, Your Grace, and what about this mongrel?" asked the crewman who had gone with him to Cragas' room.

"Keep him. He paid for the passage. He should be allowed to continue on his way."

"Aye, aye."

"You can't do that!" Cragas was fighting the crewmembers who held him fast.

"Enjoy your trip," said Thayer as he exited the ship.
***

Once Sofia was snuggled into his arms, Trenton said, "I love you, Sofia Angelina Montclair Cloverfield." He hugged her tighter. "I don't ever want to go through another day like today," he said fiercely. "And don't you make me. I will have to thrash you for days to get over the terror I felt when I thought you were gone from me forever."

Sofia lifted up. "But it wasn't my fault, Trenton. It was none of my own doing."

"Hush, darling. If you had told me the truth, I would have been able to deal with things much more efficiently, and we would not have been in this predicament." His tone was chastising. But the kiss he dropped on the top of her head was indulgent.

"Mm, I disagree, to a point. I love you too, Your Grace."

"And that is why you will marry me."

"Yes, Your Grace."

"In just over two weeks."

"Yes, Your Grace." She snuggled in even closer. He grunted his approval and hugged her tighter.

After a few moments, he said, "Sofia, I have some good news. Your father is home. He isn't dead. Neither is your mother. Robert lied." Sofia sat up quickly, bumping Trenton's chin, eliciting another grunt. This time in response to pain.

"He can't be. The letter."

"The letter you never got to read. It was a ruse to get money from the estates. Robert deceived you and your parents. It would have been ingenious if it weren't so depraved and deceitful."

"Oh. But that means... How could he... Oh." Sofia sat silently until they arrived home.

Trenton was good about allowing her time to digest the full implications of what Robert had done to her. Trenton was probably holding out the hope that Sofia would purge Robert from her life. She was confident of her protection, for she knew that Trenton would not let her brother near her after all that had happened, yet, Sofia could not understand why Robert could have ever done such a horrid thing to his family.

As they began to enter the drive, Sofia asked, "Where are they? My parents."

"Your father should be inside." Sofia boldly kissed Trenton hard as though to stake her own claim. "I believe your father sent word to your mother, but she is at a friend's home for now."

They were met at the door of the carriage by a relieved Mr. Kerns. "Milady, thank God you are safe. I will never forgive myself—"

"Never mind, Kerns. I'm safe. It wasn't your fault. There is a conspirator in your footmen that I will point out later. But don't let anyone leave."

Kerns bowed formally. "Milady."

Trenton assisted Sofia from the carriage, and if his close proximity to her person was any indication, he seemed determined to keep close for a good long time.

Once inside, she turned in the foyer to see her father and a shocked brother. "Sofia! My dear, dear girl." Her father walked to her with his arms open wide. She stepped into them.

"How did you escape? I mean, how did you find her?"

Trenton barked orders over Lord Cloverfield to have Robert removed, drawing a response from Sofia. "Your Grace, allow me to speak to him first?" She beseeched him with her tone and her pleading eyes.

"Very well, but he does not stay." She nodded. "I mean what I say, Sofia."

"Agreed." Sofia turned to stare hard at Robert.

"Yes, you might well ask why I am even here. Alive. In England. Let me tell you. The Duke of Trenton has saved me, again, from your greediness."

Robert looked down and then to the side as though he would find either an ally or a way out of the situation. "Look at me, Robert. You tell me why the note you produced wasn't real."

Robert cocked his head to the side. "Note? I believe you are unwell, for I know of no such missive."

"The note, the one that said our parents were dead. The one that you fabricated. You allowed me to mourn them, become an orphan, abandoned, and in fear of my very existence. I called His Grace some terrible names, but he isn't the bounder, you are."

Sofia shoved her brother hard, stepping after him, ramming her brother again in the chest. His only response was to step back. When Sofia took another step forward, Trenton pulled her back and stood in her way.

"Sofia, enough. This isn't talking, my love." Trenton's tone was one Sofia was familiar with, yet she disregarded it without any qualms.

"No, it is not enough, Your Grace. I won't ever forgive him. He's not a brother. He's a mongrel."

"I needed the money," said Robert, begging for understanding.

She was not going to see things his way because he had left her to a fate so horrible that she shuddered even now to think of what would have happened if Trenton had not found her.

***

Trenton had soon grown cognizant of the spectacle they were making of themselves. He spoke into the growing din of the family drama unfolding in his entryway. "Mr. Kerns, have Mrs. Kerns serve tea. Lady Sofia needs nourishment." He turned to the inhabitants of the room, his authority in his home becoming evident to all. "We will move from the entry where all and sundry can hear what is happening to the drawing room."

"Your Grace, we must return home and ease our wives' minds." Thayer instinctively matched his manner to Trenton's to allow him to retain control of an unbelievable tangle by anyone's standards.

"Yes, of course. There are no words to express my gratitude, but we will speak again soon. I have no further need to attend any balls as I have already made my choice. I have more distraction than I will ever need right here." His friends smiled and nodded. Shaking hands all around, soon Trenton's friends and partners were climbing into Thayer's coach.

Once the men had gone on their way, Trenton led the remaining two men and Sofia to the library. He had swept his little lady close to him with an arm around her middle and ignored her father's scandalized stare. The man was not at fault for what had happened, precisely, but he was at fault for raising a son that did not learn the family business. Or how to run their affairs without using the proceeds for his own ends to the detriment of his sister and family. A son who was decidedly lacking in family pride.

Sofia turned out of his arms, slipping from his grasp quickly, to stand outside the group. Her father and Trenton immediately halted, but her brother took several more steps before noticing everyone had stopped. He turned back to see the problem.

"Damn it, Sofia, will you, for once, do what you are told?"

Sofia shook her head and looked at her father, who seemed at a loss as to how he should handle his only two offspring at odds with each other and yet, there was a good reason and definite fault. She then looked to Trenton. It was to Trenton that she pled her case.

"Please, Your Grace, I am done with Robert. I have changed my mind and do not wish to hear his explanations. They mean nothing to me." She turned to look at her brother hard while speaking. "*He* means nothing to me."

Trenton moved the hair that had come out of its hastily twisted bun at some point in the preceding hours and cupped her cheek tenderly. The urge to kiss her was over-powering, and he was not in the habit of having visitors in his home when he wanted to do nothing more than ravish his woman.

"Understood," said Trenton. "I agree he has done unforgivable things, but we take care to follow the golden rule, to treat others as we would expect to be treated. Is this how I am to deal with you henceforth?"

Trenton did understand her anger. He wanted to protect her from all unpleasantness, and he could, but it would be doing his sweetheart a disservice. He wanted to shelter her, but if she didn't deal with life's problems head-on, she would find being his duchess very trying indeed.

As though she could sense his hesitancy to relent, she took the offensive. "Trenton, Your Grace, you can't compare my indiscretions to his."

Her hand went to his chest, and he didn't stop her from being familiar with him. Now was not the time to remind her of protocol and proprieties. He wanted to touch her and more besides as he stared into her eyes. They were the only two on the earth at that moment.

"Sofie, I must hear him out, my love, and so must you. You will surrender your will to mine for now. It has been a long day, and I require you to finish it so we may rest and prepare for your wedding. Your father must take possession of his home soon, so we must be done with this."

Sofie searched his eyes as he did hers. Their connection was more potent than it had ever been. She sighed. "Very well, but you may not dictate my feelings, Your Grace. I will not allow that."

"Nor would I. After you, my dear." Trenton placed his hand on the small of her back, and he was gratified when she leaned back ever so slightly. His beautiful lady.

Once they had closed the door, he placed his lady in the chair she most often frequented. Then he offered the gentlemen a drink other than tea. He waited for all to sit as he leaned against the front of his desk. He eyed the two men before he spoke.

"You may proceed. I believe you were recounting why you left your sister to die on the street," said Trenton coldly. He took a sip of his amber whiskey and sent a heated glance in Sofia's direction when she reached for the glass. So bold, confident. So damn sexy.

"You can't allow her to drink that whiskey," said her father to Trenton. "You will sit down, young lady and behave yourself. What has gotten into you? I fear it is the Duke's influence. Oh, I know he is the one they call the Devil Duke, and I am beginning to believe some of the rumors are true."

Suddenly Sofie, who was about to take a sip, released her hold on Trenton's wrist and turned swiftly, directing her blazing eyes to her father. "By all that is holy, do you not have ears in your head? Can you not comprehend my words? Do you have any idea how I was living?" demanded Sofia.

"Sofia, you will treat your father with respect." Turning incredulous eyes towards her love, she opened her mouth to speak only to find Trenton's finger on her lips. "Mind how you go, my darling."

Trenton hardened his tone and spoke with a quiet command he knew she would listen to, but he wanted to laugh at the absurdity of the situation. The man had no idea what his daughter had gone through. Well, before that good man left today, he would have the whole story.

"But he just disrespected you, Trenton. He is my father, yes, but he is not displaying any respect to others. To me." Her chest was heaving, and her breasts were teasing him. He felt his cock jerk in response.

Baron Cravenfield corrected his daughter. "Your Grace, my girl. You are speaking to a duke." She gave his rebuke no obvious consideration. One would have thought he had not spoken to her at all.

Trenton's intense gaze was one Sofia had weathered so many times before, but he knew she would respond to him. "Yes, my sweet, it was disrespectful, but he does not know me like you do. I can handle it. It will all work out, I promise you. You are to show your father due consideration," Sofia opened her mouth to respond again. Trenton shook his head, raised his eyebrow, and replaced his finger over her lips, speaking quietly. "Even if he does not earn it."

Sofia spoke through his finger in a desperate whisper as though she were begging for his agreement. "I won't."

"You will. Do I need to remind you who is in control in this house?"

She took a deep breath and released it. "No. But my family has no idea what I have been through."

"They will understand. You are not responsible for making sure they do, but you are responsible for your obedience to me."

She nodded and murmured something that the other men did not hear. However, they did hear Trenton's "Good girl" response.

Sofia turned to the two men she had grown up with and spoke as though they were simpletons. "If you do not understand, maybe I should speak more succinctly. Eight months after you left, father, I was subjected to a fabricated note saying you and mother were dead." Sofia began pacing the room. "Then, within the space of another six months, my home was sold, my possessions with it, and my brother said he was going to the continent. Not we, he. Then I find that I cannot stay with my cousin, who was the new owner, for part of the bargain was for me to leave as well." She turned to the two men who appeared to have paled in color.

"Oh, my dear, but you landed on your feet," said her father, who appeared to be clutching at straws.

Sofia graced him with a look that deemed him demented. "Imagine, I was to be turned out to the street possessing little with which to feed myself, let alone support myself. No place to lay my head, no protection for my person. And where was my elder brother? Gone." She turned her death stare to Robert.

"The lenders were out in force. They wanted the coin or me, so I had to do what was necessary to save my life."

"At the cost of your sister's life?" asked their father. The incredulity was loud now that he was beginning to see the picture.

"Oh, but there is more," continued Sofia. "I had to go to a workhouse to eat. Clerkenwell. I am sure you remember it. I can tell you the descriptors don't do it justice. That place is hell on earth. Cragas, the man who assaulted me twice and would have done unmentionable things to me if Trenton had not come early to see me and saved me, was the monster who stole me today."

"Cragas?" Robert was pale and turning green with the realization that he had bargained with the actual devil. "How was I to know?"

"Yes, the man who kidnapped me today because, according to him, he bought me from you, Robert. See, he had been trying to get to me since first discovering me in Clerkenwell. Then he was foiled on the streets where I was hiding and living, thanks to Trenton. You were so desperate for more money that leaving me destitute wasn't enough for you. You came back and sold me to a real devil."

Lord Cloverfield stood as he voiced his outrage. "Now, I can't believe Robert would do that, Sofia. It was a bad set of circumstances, to be sure, but your brother would not sell you. That only happens to women in the slums."

"Of which I was one! Bloody Hell! Have you not heard of those who lived dockside? Or St. Giles? Me!"

The room became silent after that disclosure. The truth finally seemed to have sunk in, partially. "But that could not have been true. You are over-dramatic, my girl. How did you meet the Duke of Trenton, then?"

Sofia turned desperate, tear-filled eyes to Trenton, who stood, leaving his casual leaning against his desk to open his arms. His girl had done her best, and now he would end this. It had run its course, and it was time to close this chapter of their lives.

"Sofia and I met when she was dodging the hooves of my team of bloods. She then met me again when she was discovered sleeping in my cart of wool because she was cold and tired, and that was a warm, safe place to be." He spoke tenderly as he held her tight.

Trenton ran his hand over her chilled arms and wondered where that damn tea was. He offered her his whiskey. "Sip, love. It's strong," he warned. Sofie nodded, then grimaced at the taste. "After the second attack, I demanded she come home with me, and she agreed.

"As you know, she is my ward, Lord Cloverfield, to keep her safe, and after living on the street for over two months, she has lived here for over a month. Sofia and I are to be married. Whether you protest or not, she is in agreement. But if there appears to be any hint of trouble, I have been informed, I will have no trouble getting a special license. Never doubt that a mere recounting of the reasons she was in danger, and I will have it."

The silence was uncomfortable as Lord Cloverfield digested the information. Robert was quiet, possibly hoping this moment would pass soon so he could leave.

Trenton continued. "We would like you and your wife to enjoy the wedding festivities, but that is not mandatory for the wedding to happen. It is up to you, but my Sofia is tired, hungry, and cold. I intend on taking care of all those needs and more now. You are welcome here, however, your son is not. I don't know when or if that will ever change. Only time will tell, I suppose."

The men heard and complied with his message of "time to leave" and did just that. Trenton sent them in his coach and instructed his driver to drop both men where Baron Cloverfield wanted to go. His son would find his way from there.

Turning to his betrothed, he said, "Now, show me which man in my staff has betrayed my house and what is most precious to me. On the way, we shall find out what has happened to your tea. Hmm?"

"Yes, Trenton."

"Such a good girl." He felt her shiver and smiled. There would be more of those soon.

Later that evening, when Trenton had hand-fed, bathed to the scandal of the house, and wrapped his little one in a blanket, he snuggled her in close. Sitting in front of her bedroom fire, brushing out her hair, he asked her something he needed to know.

"What would you have done if you were made to go to America on that ship?"

Sofie became animated. "Oh, I had that all worked out. I was going to tell the crew the first chance I got, which would have been soon because Cragas was already seasick just stepping onto the boat."

"Tell them what?"

She grinned. "Tell them that I was your duchess and that I was kidnapped. They would have taken care of me. Then, when we reached America, I would go to the shipping office there and make them put me on a boat back to you."

"Clever girl. But how would you have survived?"

"Trenton, really?" She leaned up and looked at Trenton. "I have my ways."

He laughed. Then he sobered. "Point well taken, my love. But henceforth, you will not use any of your unsavory talents learned while living in squalor, understood?"

"I'll try to resist the urge." She smiled.

"And curb that tongue of yours. I foresee a few spanking occasions surrounding that tongue."

"Yes, sir." She tried to sound contrite, but Trenton only shook his head at her lack of conviction. "Did you deal with that footman?"

Trenton sighed. "I did, and that is all I will say on that subject." He left no doubt as to the seriousness of his statement.

"And did you dispose of the tutor?"

"God, yes, with a reference and wage she didn't earn, but it was worth it to be rid of her."

Sofie giggled and looked up at him mischievously. "I do love you, Trenton, even if you try to force me to do things I do not want to do."

He sighed. "Like the tutor."

"Yes, and the guardianship. I thought you didn't want me, and that was your way of helping me but ending our playtimes."

"It was because I was so tempted and didn't think I should force you if you didn't want to be with me. I could prevent anyone else claiming your heart if I had to agree to the alliance. I love you, my mouthy woman." She lifted her face for his kiss.

"Time for bed. Soon you'll sleep in my chambers."

"Oh, Your Grace, that is scandalous."

"It is, isn't it? It is my house, remember." Trenton swooped in for another kiss.

"Oh," she panted, "I remember."

Epilogue

The wedding guests were gone, and the anticipation that had Sofia tingling all morning was exacerbated by Trenton touching her intimately often. He held her hand and hugged her. He even kissed her cheek in front of others, but what they didn't see was the hand on her thigh under the table. The patting of her bottom and his manhood bumping up against her backside. His hand brushed her breast when he was dancing with her. All very taboo and so deliciously naughty, she was ready to burst into erotic flames.

"Shall we slip into something easier to breathe in, my darling duchess?" He cocked his eyebrow in the most decadent way sending chills down her spine and deep into her core.

"Darling Duchess. I do like the sound of that, but I shouldn't use it at formal affairs."

"Too much?" His grin had an evil tilt as he pulled Sofie into his arms, kissing her.

"I suppose we should have a façade of propriety for those not within our circle of friends. Now, I've changed my mind. No changing. Just remove your clothes and remain bare. Tonight, my love, I will change your perception of pleasure forever."

"Again?"

"Minx. I love you, Sofia Angelina, Duchess of Trenton."

"And I, you, my Devil Duke."

The End

About the Author
Alyssa Bailey

USA Today and #1 Bestselling Author of Diverse Romance that is realistic and sensual with a touch of suspense. A dyed in the wool Texan living in Alaska for half her life, Alyssa now divides her time between the beauty of Southeast Alaska and the piney woods of East Texas. She enjoys taking from her own experiences to create series in fictitious worlds sure to tease the reader's palate and invite them to sink into exciting adventures.

Alyssa enjoys writing consensual power exchanges between intelligent, sassy women who are not afraid to make a stand and loving men confident enough to give his woman space but masterful enough to keep her safe despite her choices. There is *always* a happily ever after.

Visit me online and sign up for my Newsletter:
http://alyssabailey.com

Join my Facebook Group for fun and prizes:
https://www.facebook.com/alyssabailey.romance

Other Romance Books by Alyssa Bailey

Lords and Little Ladies: Regency Historical, Spicy
Lord Thayer's Choice
Lord Ashton's Decision
The Black Laird Requires
Lord Kendrick's Obligation

Darling Duchesses: Regency, Daddy Dom, Spicy
The Devil Duke's Little Distraction

Chase Abbey Series: Regency, Spicy, Suspense
Lord Barrington's Minx
Becoming Lady Barrington
Lady Caroline's Defiance
His Improper Lady

Safe and Secure Series: Contemporary, Suspense, Spicy
Saving Sharlee
Saving Jessie

Safe and Secure II: Contemporary, Suspense, Spicy
Saving Ivy
Securing Mallory (2021)
Securing Becky (2021)
Securing Finley (TBD)
Securing Callie (TBD)

The O'Connor Series: Contemporary, Rancher, DD, Spicy

    Liam & Jocelyn's Story-
    Her Sweet Complication
    Liam's Lessons
    Loving Liam

    Ciarán and Katherine's Story
    His Gentle Persuasion
    Rancher's Creed
    Katie Consents

    Quinlan and Cheyenne's Story
    Quinlan's Quest
    Accepting His Way
    Her Balancing Act

    Kelli and Parker's Story
    Meeting Her Needs
    Kissing Kelli
    Keeping Kelli

    Cián and Molly's Story
    In Pursuit of Molly
    Freeing Molly
    Forever Molly

Lone Wind Series: Contemporary, Spicy, Native American

    Reclaiming Clover

Clearwater Ranch Trilogy -Contemporary, Spicy, Alpha
   Piper's Plan
   Camille's Second Chance
   Josie's Refuge

Taming Texanna-American Historical, Native American, Spicy
   Cowboy Welcome- Contemporary, Spicy
   In the Spirit of Christmas -Contemporary, Sweet

   Red Eagle Ranch- Contemporary, Rancher, Spicy, Multi-Cultural
   Stryker's Girl (Book 1)

Guardians of Refuge- Contemporary, Military, Spicy
   SEAL of Refuge (Book 1)
   The Strategy of Love (Book 2)
   The Tactics of Love (Book 3)

Anthologies (Heat Varies)

Sweet Town Love
Historical Heroes
Hero to Obey (limited time)
Cowboy for a Cause (limited time)

Multi-Author Box Sets (Heat Level Various)
Love, Christmas 2 Movies You Love
Love, Christmas 2 Recipes
FREE Book Bites 11

Christmas Shorts
Irresistible Heroes
Tempting Protectors
Sexy and Seductive
Sweet and Sassy Summertime Vol. 2
Dear Santa: A Christmas Wish
Sweet and Sassy New Beginnings (July 20, 2021)